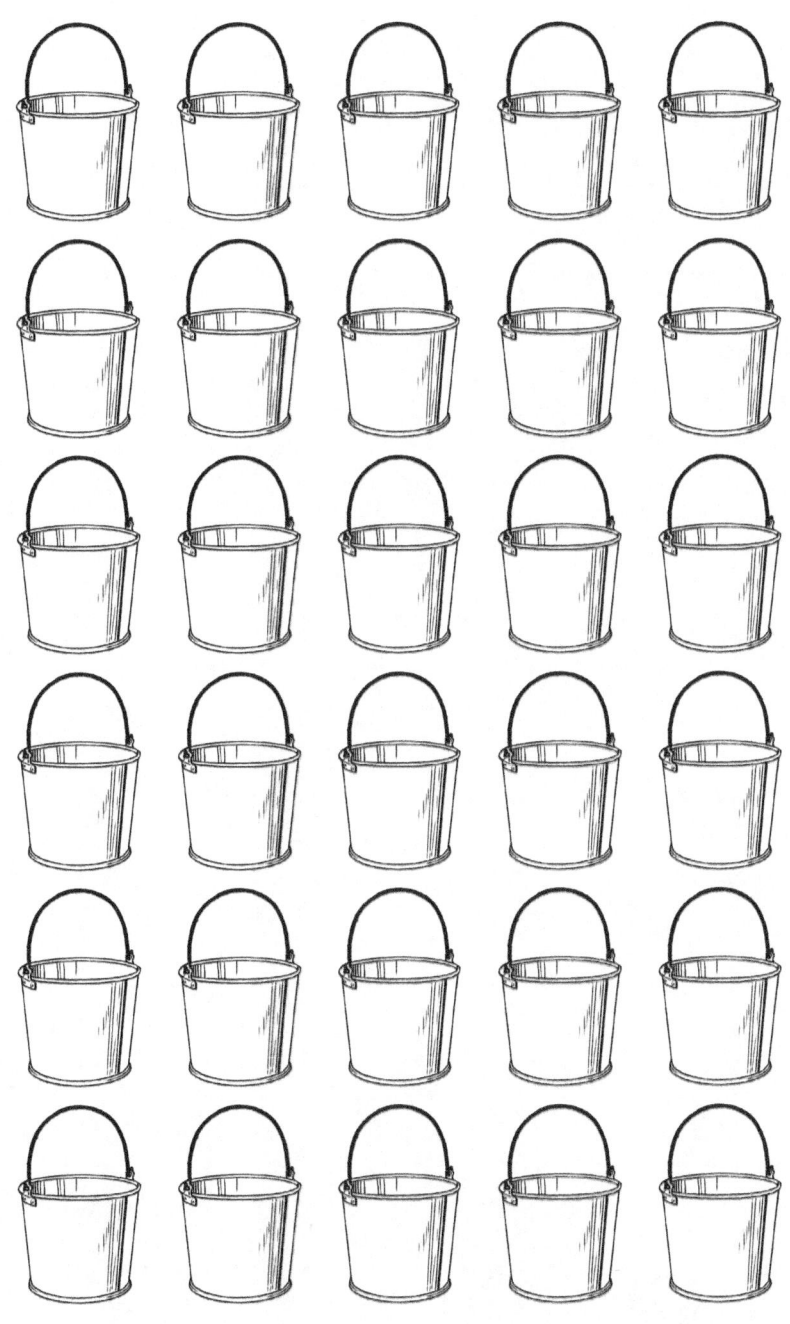

Pure Slush Books

2014

November

Vol. 11

a Pure Slush book

Pure
Slush

2014 November Vol. 11 is edited by Matt Potter and
published by Pure Slush, September 2014.

All stories are copyright © of the individual authors

Front cover photograph copyright © Nick Lobeck
http://8am.ch

ISBN: 978—1—925101—53—9

You can find *Pure Slush* at http://pureslush.webs.com

Copies of all *Pure Slush* publications can be bought
at http://pureslush.webs.com/store.htm

All queries re *Pure Slush* can be made
via email to edpureslush@live.com.au

A note on differences in punctuation and spelling

Pure Slush proudly features (both online and in print) writers from all over the English—speaking world. Some speak and write English as their first language, while for others, it's their second or third or even fourth language. Naturally, across all versions of English, there are differences in punctuation and spelling, and even in meaning. These differences are reflected in the stories *Pure Slush* publishes, and it accounts for any differences in punctuation, spelling and meaning found within these pages.

stories by

Guilie Castillo–Oriard	James Claffey
Townsend Walker	Gwendolyn Joyce Mintz
Derek Osborne	Stephen V. Ramey
Gloria Garfunkel	Gay Degani
John Wentworth Chapin	Sally–Anne Macomber
Lynn Beighley	Mandy Nicol
Andrew Stancek	Margaret Bingel
Rachel Ambrose	Darryl Price
Gill Hoffs	Teresa Burns Gunther
Susan Tepper	Matt Potter
Jessica McHugh	Gary Percesepe
Shane Simmons	Nathaniel Tower
Michelle Elvy	Kimberlee Smith
Len Kuntz	Vanessa Weibler Paris
Michael Webb	Joanne Jagoda

The Inevitable
by Guilie Castillo—Oriard

Saturday, 1ˢᵗ November 2014

There's something biblical about downpours in Curaçao. Rain crashes down in windblown sheets that whip water in directions that defy gravity, into puddles that become ponds, that become white—crested lagoons.

Luis's porch — ex—porch, now — is slick with water. The sliding doors are beaded with splash, even under the porch roof. The saline lake down below, the cacti—and—scraggly—bush landscape that greeted him every morning, now sports fringes of vibrant green.

It won't last, Luis knows. As soon as the rain season is over — January, maybe February if the island's lucky — the sun will bake the green back into withered brown. He saw it happen during his first months here. And now he's leaving before it happens again.

The click of a lock disengaging, and the front door opens with its usual dragging catch on the front step. So easy to fix: he would've done it himself if he'd had a sander.

Marjan walks into the hall shaking out her hair, leaving wet footprints. He has no right to be annoyed. Luis is here to turn in his keys. She and Vikram, his neighbors — ex—neighbors — have taken on the administration of the condos. "Sorry I'm late. Vikram had a flat on the Emancipatie Boulevard, and you know how bad that floods." She barks laughter, and Luis thinks of Al. Not that he needs special prompts to do that. The dog's absence has emptied Luis's life.

"I just got here, too."

Marjan keeps up a steady commentary – about the weather, the island government fiascos, the injustice of Vikram being unable to take vacation in December: "People with kids get priority; it's discrimination, pure and simple" – as she follows him upstairs into the master bedroom and bath, guest bedroom and bath, back downstairs to the laundry room, living room, kitchen. His cleaning lady did a good job. Great, in fact. When Marjan opens the refrigerator, Luis gets a whiff of chilled lemon–scent Disiclin.

"Looks like you did my job for me." Marjan looks around, nods, presumably happy. "The new tenant could move in today."

"It's been rented? Already?" He didn't expect this twinge of loss.

"You kidding? These condos go like fresh stroopwafels at the Haarlem market. Especially towards the end of the year. All you corporate guys move at the same time, apparently."

He doesn't know what to say. His stuff is packed; two suitcases in the hotel room he'll call home until his flight on Tuesday, three boxes at the movers' warehouse. The house he lived in for eleven months has been washed and cleaned of him, his presence, his life. Why, then, does it still feel so *his*?

But Marjan isn't waiting for a reply. "Must be so exciting. Every few years a new country, new people, new weather ..." She looks up from the documents she's paging through on the polished concrete of the kitchen counter. "Though – London you said, eh? You could've waited for spring."

No, he couldn't, even though Srikantha, his old college buddy and now his new boss, told him – the kind of for–your–college–buddy's–ears–only thing he probably regretted as soon as he said it – that Management was so elated they'd wait as long as it took. But Luis was eager, too. Everything about Curaçao screamed his failures back at him, steel claws on a blackboard everywhere he looked, everything he did. Every memory he had.

Marjan scrawls out an IOU for the security deposit. He'll drop it off at the office on his way back to the hotel. He turned in his keycard yesterday, before his farewell happy hour, but Saturdays are busy at Ehrlich Curaçao. Someone will let him in.

Maybe he'll just slip it into the mailbox. Avoid a second round of goodbyes.

"So …" Marjan says at the front door in that unique, drawn-out way the Dutch have, which always reminds Luis of Maria teaching the von Trapp children the notes on an Austrian mountaintop. "Enjoy your trip, and much success in London." She gives him the three standard Dutch pecks on the cheeks – *three, because they're free* – and pats his shoulder in an awkward pseudo-hug.

"Thank you. For – well, for all your help."

"Graag gedaan. Doei!" She waves and disappears back into the house. The front door catches with a muffled scrape before slamming closed.

He should've borrowed a sander.

His black Wrangler Rubicon is, of course, gone. It lasted three whole days after Al left with Pélagie. He told the carwash guys he'd give them each fifty guilders if they got every last dog hair out, and after he drove it straight to the dealer's second-hand lot. He has a rental now, a white automatic Kia sedan that smells of too many people and cheap something-berry deodorizer, that feels too low on the road, that lacks the Jeep's grace in everything from windshield wiper action to the silky suede of its upholstery.

Which is, in fact, the point.

And yet, even a car without memories is capable of reading a driver's mind. Luis doesn't remember making a left instead of a right on the Caracasbaaiweg; he doesn't remember any of the other turns he must have made to get away from the shops and traffic lights and into the wild, thorny clusters of the *mondi*. He doesn't remember any conscious thought, in fact, until the tires bump down onto rutted dirt and his right foot, working on instinct, steps off the accelerator to work the brake. When his left foot pumps air instead of a clutch pedal, when his right hand grabs for the Jeep's sleek gearshift and finds instead the clammy plastic of the Kia's handbrake – that's when he returns from wherever he was and looks up in time to see the sign before the car passes under it: Sint Joris Baai.

The dog beach.

Fuck.

Even if Pélagie hadn't forbidden all contact, not just with her but – especially – with Al. Even if Luis didn't wholeheartedly agree that a clean break was the only way to go, the only way to help Al – Luis himself – move forward. It's freakin' *raining*. More of a drizzle now, but still. Pélagie wouldn't bring her dogs, any dog, out in this weather. Al is safe, dry, on a pile of blankets, in an extra–large basket, somewhere in a corner of Pélagie's house. This is the absolute last place Al would be found today.

The dirt road is too narrow to turn the car around. He drives on, gut feeling like a misshapen cat's cradle, until the road widens, the gray–green of the bay fills the windshield, the tires crunch more sand than dirt – and he sees the impossible: Pélagie's red Explorer, muddy as always, parked by the makeshift benches.

No sign of her, though. Or of dogs. Luis can turn around and leave without ever being seen. Drive back to town, to the Ehrlich building, to his hotel; brush up on UK statutes and treaties, keep marking time in the limbo his life has become, until Tuesday and the airport and the plane and leaving all this –

failure, heartbreak, disappointment – behind. Start over. Sluice that slate down.

He parks alongside the Explorer. He was right: it's empty.

Outside, the air smells raw, like just–picked mushrooms. The fading rain polka–dots his shirt and kisses his face, his arms. It makes the flat surface of the bay whisper; a *sshhh* that feels more like commiseration than admonition.

There they are. In a replay of the scene from April – exactly, he realizes with a sensation of fateful intervention, seven months ago – Pélagie is walking along the curve of the bay. She might even be wearing the same clothes: the dark yoga pants, the loose green tank top. This time, though, there's only one dog with her. The only dog possible.

Al lopes quietly, leashless, by Pélagie's side. He was always far ahead of Luis, running back and forth: faster, Human, faster! Sniffing here and there and oh, over there! Now the dog's head hangs steady, incurious, except when he looks up at Pélagie every few steps. Looking for guidance. Making sure she's still there?

The landscape blurs; it's the wind, dust in his eyes. He swipes at them. Drive away, dammit. Before –

Too late. Al's head comes up, sniffing, looking this way. Then – just like April, but in the opposite direction – the dog is off, sprinting like a cheetah, wet sand lifting in tufts behind him. Pélagie whistles – at least Luis assumes it's her, because his eyes are glued to the black giant barreling toward him – but the dog doesn't slow. Then the dunes cut off Luis's view. In seven seconds Al will be over the top, three more and he'll be all over Luis.

Get in the car.

Luis leans against the Kia, bracing himself. For the weight of Al's wet, sandy body. For the wrath he'll incur from Pélagie. For the consequences. For the inevitable.

La Ronde / Alexei and Frank
by Townsend Walker

Sunday, 2nd November 2014

Morning dawns late, but brightly. By nine, the night storm clears and the sun creates sparklers in the new snow in Central Park. Alexei's kids, Sasha and Ivan, have been up for hours, planning their day in the Park. Alexei stumbles to the nook where Sally has laid out her Sunday morning breakfast: breads and jams (all homemade and sweet) and coffee. He's greeted by a chorus of, "When can we go to the park? You said we could go early, before the snow all melts."

These American kids of his do not understand how sick of snow he is; growing up in Leningrad, it was something to be managed, not played in. Snow covered the ground for at least a third of the year and the temperature never got above −7C. He's the one who has to play with them. Sally, who grew up in Charleston, never lasts more than fifteen minutes outside and has no clue about how to build a good snowman, or even a bad one. Last year through some preternatural intuition she managed to have her mother or father sick just before every major storm when *I just have to be with them. No telling what my sister Clarisse would do. Never had a responsible bone in her body, that girl.*

That's the period Alexei picked up mistress #2, Corinne, at Rose Bar. And now can't seem to shake her. Away from her, he

18

thought he should; lying next to her naked he didn't think, so the twain is never broken.

The kids skip around the breakfast table, tug on their father's sleeve, clamoring to go. Alexei gulps his coffee, takes a shower, dresses, dons a parka and his ushanka, and walks Sasha and Ivan to the Great Lawn. "Go build a snowman." Sits down on a nearby bench. His mobile buzzes; it's Corinne.

"What's my sweetie doing this morning?"

"Watching his kids make a snowman in the park, and you?"

"Keeping everything warm for you. You want me to describe what's being kept toasty?"

"I don't think I could handle that on a park bench."

"We still on for two?"

"Best I know. Sally's taking the kids to a birthday party for one of Ivan's classmates."

Alexei looks up at his children. "Hey Ivan! Gotta go, Corinne, Ivan's swinging a branch at Sasha."

The kids have been fumbling around trying to get their snowman started. Alexei stands up, falls in the snow, stretches his arms out, gathers a mass of it into a ball, rolls it one way, then another, pats it round, rolls again. "See, that's how it's done." He walks back to the bench.

"Alexei, that you?" A man walking on the path with two kids in tow, looks vaguely familiar, tall, gold sunglasses, Mets ball cap, long coat down to his ankles.

"It's Frank, remember we met a couple of weeks ago at the risk management conference?"

"Now I do. It was the glasses that threw me."

"These are my kids, Molly and Lance. Say hello to Mr. Mendelev."

"Mine are over there making a snowman. You want to help?"

The kids are introduced to one another and the boys figure out they'll do the heavy lifting and the girls are delegated to

19

decorate the snowman when they're finished. Frank and Alexei retire to the bench.

"Where did you get those shades?"

"You like them? CliC Gold, 75K."

"What?"

"When I called the Comcast / Time Warner deal right, and in size, management felt they ought to show appropriate appreciation, in addition to the bonus of course."

"Bravo, how did you figure it out? We got stuck with some bad paper, not large, but we took a bit of a hit."

"Not the kind of thing I can talk about, but I did hear something last week about our phone company. I wouldn't want to be holding anything with their name on it come next week."

"Thanks."

Frank and Alexi look over to where their kids are making bigger and bigger balls for the snowman.

"They won't be lifting those things up."

"Hey, I only see three kids there. Where's Lance?" Frank shouts. "Lance! Lance!" Alexei looks at Frank wondering what the panic is about. The boy pops up from behind the largest ball of snow.

"That reminds me of something I heard a while back. This guy, works on the street apparently, with a price on his head. Big, I'm told, like a quarter mil."

"Didn't know it took that much to get a job done. Maybe we're in the wrong business."

"Guess it does. Not much of a description on the guy, tall, maybe works for you, Prada aviators, loses his kids in the park sometimes."

"Why would anyone want to kill a banker? Let me rephrase that: why would anyone need to be paid to off a banker?"

"What I heard, it's the wife wants him gone. "

Frank is quiet for a moment, then, "Seems a bit harsh, just because he loses the kids. But what a great story it makes."

"And runs around on her, but hey, who doesn't?"

20

Frank seems to disconnect from the conversation: turns to look at a young couple jogging down the path; watches some squirrels scamper in the trees; shifts his focus to the kids. "Looks like we need to help them put this snowman together."

The two adults and four kids assemble a six−foot snowman. The fathers hold up their daughters so they decorate the face with twigs and pinecones and candy (Molly found a sucker in her pocket). Smart phone pics are snapped of the kids and the snowman. They split, one east, one west to go home.

Gone about ten yards when Alexei yells out, "Thanks for the phone tip."

Walking back to his apartment on West 79th, Alexei starts thinking about Frank. *Those sunglasses. Last time he wasn't wearing those gold ones, but Prada Aviators, blue tint. Is this the guy Lana was looking for? Sure fits what she told me: tall, head of M&A at Goldman. And he panicked when he thought his kid had gotten lost.*

Pulls out his cell: "Lana sweetie, your little brother has come through. Frank Cabot, head of M&A at Goldman. Go for it. Oh, and don't forget our deal."

"Daddy, you talk to Aunt Lana? Tell her to come see us."

"I will, honey."

Frank walks back to his apartment on Park Avenue, the conversation with Alexei buzzing in his head. *He was talking about me. Me. Madge has a contract out on me − that bitch!* He kicks at a clump of snow piled up on the sidewalk.

"Daddy, be careful, you're getting me all wet."

"Sorry, Molly−kins."

No wonder she's been so complaisant lately.

He begins to sing Hook's Tarantella from *Peter Pan* and skips along with Molly and Lance.

Oh, what joy to see her face when the tables turn. It will be slow. It will hurt.

Rebirth
by Derek Osborne

Monday, 3rd November 2014

*I*t's OK, Becca, you don't need to stay.

The last two weeks have been rough. Max has been in a lot of pain. They've hooked up a morphine pump so he can self–medicate. Rebecca has also been in a great deal of discomfort. The baby is restless. The entire family is now standing ready. Max's two older daughters have flown in, kids in tow, and Rebecca's younger sister, Consuela, is also there. Nantucket is now the bleak, blue, scrub–brushed sand dune it was when the first fisherman built fires there two centuries ago. The grand cedar cottages fade into gray winter skies. The wind brings with it a special chill, the kind only the Atlantic in November can know.

Really, hun, go lie down.

Max is no longer sure if he is speaking or imagining.

There's really no difference, is there?

He senses another presence now, one that hears whatever he says.

"How is he?" Andi asks, coming back inside from the patio. She needed some air. "How are you, for that matter?"

"I am fine," Rebecca says.

"Why don't you go lay down."

Yes, that's right Andi, maybe she'll listen to you.

"Will you stay with him?"

"Of course."

Rebecca grabs the rail of the bed to hoist herself up. She's no longer wearing the cast.

"Oh God."

"What is it?" Max whispers, finding the will to speak. He tries to open his eyes. "What's wrong?"

"Hold on, Dad," Andi says.

"My water broke."

"It can't, it's too early," Andi says.

"Well, what do you call that?"

Andi looks down at the floor where Rebecca is standing. A small puddle is seeping under the bed, dripping down the leg of the chair.

"Oh God!" Andi screams. "Senora Vasquez! Senora Vasquez!"

"Ma!" Rebecca chimes in.

There is a look people get when they know they are walking into chaos. For a strong woman like Senora Vasquez it is a look that says okay, I am in control, I know what to do, everything will be fine; but just beneath, the panic lurks, waiting to pop, waiting to burst like a bomb. "Get to your bed," she says, waving a hand.

"Isn't she early?" Andi says.

"Anja?" la senora calls out, "Call the clinic."

La senora knows what to do, Andi. Everything's fine. So he's a little early. The kid already survived a six foot fall. What's a little premature daylight? Kinda funny, eh Maggie? Remember Andi? How she turned and sat straight up in that final hour? I thought the doctor handled it well.

Max has been having visitors all week, some real, some imagined. They come to sit with him, come to say their goodbyes. Maggie, his first wife, who also died of cancer, has been a regular.

This is not a drill. Repeat, this is not a drill.

24

Max is smiling. Andi notices.

"What are you smiling at?"

She'll be fine, Andi. You can go be with her if you want. I'll just lie here and listen.

"How is everyone?" Pam says, entering the room. She was upstairs taking a nap. She sees the kids have all gathered in the hall, struggling to get a view.

"Get them out!" la senora snaps. "Anja, have you called the doctor?"

"They're getting him," she hears Anja yell from in the kitchen.

Rebecca looks over at Max. A rare flood of sunlight filters in through the French doors that line the harbor side of the house. The room is radiant. They have set Max up in what was the living room. Rebecca is still on the porch. They're getting her settled onto the bed. She glances over at Andi and then back to Max. Andi presses her hands together by the side of her head. He's sleeping. Rebecca smiles at the curious children. They'll remember this day. Right then the first of the contractions come.

"Whoa!" Rebecca says, catching her breath.

"You are already dilating. This child is in a hurry," la senora says. "Anja, where is that doctor?"

"He's on his way," comes the voice again.

"Aye, cunjo," Rebecca groans when the next contraction comes.

You'll be fine, Becca, you'll be fine. Won't she, Mags? Why don't you go over and take a peek? We're old pros at this, aren't we? Kind of glad I'm not over there. Remember Mike and Marsha when Sam was born? She jacked him right off the floor and screamed, 'You did this to me!' Don't think I've ever laughed so hard in my life. Yeah, I remember you didn't share my humor. But Becca's strong, she'll be fine, won't she? Why don't you take a look?

"Dad, are you trying to say something? It's Andi, I'm right here."

25

She's been watching his face, lips parting as if to speak, then going back to that same hint of a smile. He seems peaceful enough. Through the doors leading out to the porch, across the gray empty harbor, she can see the flashing red lights of the ambulance winding its way through the village. They've all been so helpful, everyone, people showing up with covered dishes, even Betty, the neighbor, who is probably a billionaire from selling balloons and party favors out of her fifteen hundred stores, who's been coming once a week to disinfect the kitchen and rooms where Rebecca and Max sleep ... everyone. "I started out cleaning floors," she said that first day. "I still clean my own house." *Gadabout* sits at her mooring, alone, the docks dismantled, only the orange Coast Guard cutter across the way for company, her bow facing the house as if she, too, is waiting. A potential buyer is supposed to come out this Friday. They haven't told Max.

Breathe Becca, breathe into it. Bend to it. How's she doin' *Mags? Talk to her. Go and whisper, tell her I'm still here, tell her* *I'm not leaving, not yet.*

Max can hear the siren coming down the road. His old friend, Tommy, has entered the room. He's standing now at the foot of the bed. "Tom," Max whispers. Andi leans down.

"What did you say?"

"Tommy's here."

Max struggles to open his eyes.

"Tom? You mean Uncle Tommy?"

"What's he saying?" Rebecca calls from the other room. She can see Andi leaning over the bed.

"I'm not sure. I think he's hallucinating."

Tommy's here, Andi, he's right there at the foot of the bed. *Your Mom is here too. Tell her Mags, tell her you're here.*

"Daddy, Tommy's not here."

But he is, hun.

The doctor walks in with a nurse, two paramedics stand out in the hall. Rebecca likes him, he looks like a doctor, small and

26

thin, balding on top, wire rim glasses, nice Jewish face. "Who called Central Casting?" she says as he enters. It's been their little joke.

"Oh, I forgot my cap," the nurse says. She is also straight out of Central Casting.

"We're laughing," the doctor says, "we're laughing. This is a good thing." He walks over to check on Max. "How's the big guy?"

"He's pretty out of it."

The doctor lifts one of Max's eyelids, takes his pulse, placing a hand gently on his forehead. He's learned long ago not to show his thoughts, but he's grown close to this little group, this mix of old and new. Andi is searching the doctor's face. He pushes his glasses back up his nose. "You stay close, Andi, I've got to be with Rebecca. Hold his hand. Let him know you're here." The others are watching, listening. For a moment the room grows quiet. The children can sense it, the older hushing the little ones. They crowd at the portico straining to see. "So, this one is in a hurry," the doctor says, pulling Rebecca's sheet to the foot of the bed. "Children in the kitchen." This over his shoulder. They scamper. Doctors mean business.

"Shouldn't we take her to the clinic?" la senora says.

He looks about the room, the long wall of delicate doors, white linen drapes touching the gray slate floor, *Gadabout* standing close by. "No, she's a little early but last week everything looked fine." He's moving his stethoscope over Rebecca's belly. "I've got the bus right outside." He takes a quick glance toward the other room, then speaks directly to la senora. "This is a good place."

Thanks, Doc.

"OK, folks, let's clear the room. Rebecca, you're already dilating. It all looks good. Let's get this baby born."

Go for it, Becca, bring him now. We've already talked about this. I'm sorry I won't be here, I'm sorry I won't be able to help you through all those times when you'll need me. Find a good man. I mean that. When Maggie told me to find a good woman I never thought it could happen and then, there you were ...

Max can hear the sounds of labor. He should be used to them now, but he's not.

I'm still with you on everything we spoke of. I just thought by now I'd have figured it out. I thought at least I'd be able to leave you with some final wisdom. Isn't that what's supposed to happen? Maybe that's it, the grand illusion, there is no answer, only the wonder and majesty. Maybe that's what Gadabout was trying to show me, no home to come back to, only the journey, the joy of the journey.

He hears the doctor coaching, Anja's words of encouragement.

You have been my greatest joy. That night we drove home from the restaurant ... sitting on my lap all the way ... That's not a betrayal, Mags, it was just that I knew by then every moment was borrowed, every moment, even when we fought I cherished you. Every second with you, Becca.

The sounds are growing distant. His old friend, Tommy, stands by the foot of the bed, his hand outstretched. The room has filled with light.

Not yet, Tom, not yet.

Rebecca's cries sound stronger.

I've tried to tell you all the stories, all the important ones, ask the others, I'm sure there're a few I've forgotten. Tell them to Max. Get him into a boat, sooner than later. A boat is a great way to build confidence ... Don't cry ... I can hear your cries ... It's beautiful, Becca, it's beautiful ... and I am not frightened of dying. Fitting, don't you think? I've had such a good life. Maggie and Tommy are here. They're here to help. They're here ... they're all here ...

"Push Rebecca!"

"Daddy, he's coming!"

"Push Rebecca. One more time."

Is that him?

"Max, we have a son!"

The others are silent. Newborn cries pierce the light.

"Daddy? Daddy don't go …"

"Max?" Rebecca calls.

Andi is lifting her father's hand to kiss.

"Max?"

The baby's cries fill the room. The doctor is placing him onto her chest. Andi looks over, smiling through tears.

"Oh Max."

Into the light, and into the light.

An Early Thanksgiving
by Gloria Garfunkel

Tuesday, 4th November 2014

I started to wonder how to get through Thanksgiving. We decided to celebrate it unconventionally early, yesterday, with just part of the family. I was in an OK mood but didn't want to go anywhere and stayed glued to the TV watching *Law and Order: Special Victims Unit*. I love Detective Munch. He's my kind of cynical, paranoid Jew obsessed with conspiracies. I had my sister's family over for a low−key vegetarian feast she cooked for me. I can't stand to kill a bird for a Holiday.

We were just sitting down to eat. Phone rings.

"Your father died in a car accident. One car," said my brother−in−law Mitch, blanching. "The funeral is tomorrow."

I'm not surprised. This is one of his many one−car crashes. He's been in and out of psych units with Bipolar 1 my whole life and has made various suicide attempts. If Chloe and I had kids together, they wouldn't have a fighting chance.

Chloe has stayed up with me all night and into the morning, baking me brownies and brewing me tea. I'm in numb mode. I don't feel a thing. It's like he wasn't my father at all, even though we talked to each other about how work is going on the phone every Sunday afternoon. He lived in New Jersey and I'm in Massachusetts. I have all these flashes in my mind of what he looked like at different ages and bipolar moods, from violence to hilarity.

Jade

by John Wentworth Chapin

Wednesday, 5th November 2014

When Charles gets back to work, there's only a pair of older women shopping in Eastern Antiques. His father, Chuck, is there, unpacking a shipment, and Deonna is nowhere to be seen. The two men nod at each other, more like co-workers than estranged father and son. Dealing with shipments and new merchandise is generally Charles' job, but he hates it, so he settles himself behind the cash register. Chuck crashed on Charles' couch for about four days after he arrived out of the blue, and then moved on to Deonna's place. Charles is both mortified at the whole situation and a little impressed that his father can weasel his way into situations like this so well. Problem: If he's living with her sleeping with her, what's to say that Deonna doesn't decide that it's not worth it to pay Charles anymore when she can have Chuck for free – and out the door goes Charles? He hasn't had the heart to tell Deonna about his father's no–good–ness. It's embarrassing to tell people that your father stole from you, and there's a certain amount of the–apple–doesn't–fall–too–far–from–the–tree that Charles worries about. If his father is a lout, doesn't that sort of imply that he's a lout, too – or at least put people on wary notice? If they know about his father, it seems to Charles he'll have to work extra hard to distance himself from the bad. Easier to keep it quiet.

"I'm thinking of moving," Charles announces to Chuck. In a big, antiqued mirror with flecks of algal green, he watches Chuck work, unpacking trinkets.

"Where?" Chuck asks.

"Not sure," Charles answers, shrugging.

"Moving is a pain in the ass," Chuck says.

"Nothing keeping me here," Charles replies.

Chuck squints at his son with one eye. "You can move around all you like, and there's nothing wrong with it. But leaving isn't going to do you an ounce of good if the problem's not where you live but who you are."

"Thanks, Chuck. Good to know."

"I hate that sarcastic shit. Say what you mean. The whole goddamned world is sarcastic nowadays. It's weak."

Charles says, "Thank you for telling me I'm damaged and weak." He glances at the two women shopping; his father strikes him as grubby and low–class.

"You're being sarcastic."

"I don't know how to be anything else, Chuck."

Chuck is silent, and Charles spies him lifting a cat figurine and peering into it. Then Chuck steals a sideways glance at Charles, unaware that Charles is watching him in the mirror. He fishes a small plastic bag from up inside the cat and tucks it quickly into his back left pocket, eyes darting back to Charles.

Ah. And there we have it, Charles thinks.

"Well, sarcasm isn't good for you. But move if you want. It's no skin off my nose. Hey, where do think Dee wants this?" Chuck indicates to Charles the dark green porcelain cat in his hand, and then he walks all the way across the store to Charles and hands it to him. "This one looks like it's worth something," he says. "Probably should go someplace special."

Charles looks at the cat carelessly, trying not to seem too interested in it, casually rolling it over and noting that the inside is hollow and empty. He holds it up to the light. "There's nothing special about it," he says.

"Dee!" Chuck calls.

Deonna appears moments later in the doorway to the back office, her crazy hair pulled down in wisps around her face. "What?"

"I'm helping Charles unpack," Chuck says. "Where would you want that green cat?"

Charles feels the room roll away from him, like he's on the deck of a pitching yawl in a storm.

Dee is irritated by the question. "Lord, Charles, help your old man out. That goes with all the other cats." Then she stops. She wrinkles her brow and steals a glance at the two women shoppers making their way to the exit.

"Goodbye, ladies. C'mon back soon now," Deonna says.

She looks back at Charles, her eyes ablaze. She strides across the store to Charles' perch behind the register, and she takes the cat from him. She turns her back to Charles. Charles watches two things in the mirror: Deonna reaching into the cat with two fingers and Chuck watching Deonna.

Deonna stands upright and walks the cat to a glass shelf, where she sets it next to the other green porcelain cats and frogs.

"I want to see you in the back, Charles," she says, voice brittle. She disappears through the doorway into the office. Charles follows her, watching Chuck watch it all.

In the office, Deonna whips around to face him, inches from his face. She lays her hand out expectantly, her jaw set tight and grim.

Charles looks at her hand and looks at her.

"What?" he says, stupidly.

"Fork it over," she demands.

"Fork what over?" Charles asks.

The expectant hand shoots out and slaps him, hard, on the cheek. It makes a louder sound than he would have expected. She's wearing heavy rings that hurt his jaw.

"What the fuck!" Charles exclaims, his hand coming up too late to defend himself.

Deonna hisses, "Don't fuck with me. Give me the bag."

"I don't have any bag," Charles says. "Go ask your boyfriend."

Deonna moves to slap him again, but Charles grabs her wrist before she can hit him.

"It's pretty goddamned low to blame your own father for your own shitty behavior," she says. "Now hand it over." She tries to pull her arm from his grasp, but Charles holds her firmly.

"I don't have anything," Charles says. "I don't even know what you're talking about."

"Let go of me," she says, trying to pull away.

Charles clamps her wrist more firmly. Suddenly, her other hand shoots out at him in a fist, and Charles raises his other arm to ward off her blow. A sharp pain bursts from his forearm, and he hears a brittle snap. She has stabbed him with a pencil. An inch of broken pencil protrudes from his arm in a growing circle of blood.

She yells at him, screaming and cussing while she beats at him with her free hand. He's warding off the blows with his bleeding arm. Then Charles feels himself pushed sideways, two hands clamped on his bleeding arm. He sprawls sideways and lets go of Deonna's arm as he tries to stop from falling. He crashes against the tall antique green filing cabinet where Deonna keeps all her invoices. He catches himself on her desk with a flailing hand and turns to see his father and Deonna both glowering at him.

"Give it to me, you little fucking faggot," Deonna hisses.

Charles looks to his father to see his reaction, but the man has an incredible poker face. Either that, or he feels nothing.

"Give you what?" Charles asks. He has a piece of paper stuck to the blood on his forearm, and he notices that the pencil nub is still stuck into him, the rest of the pencil dangling by a splinter.

She scowls. "You know what I mean."

Charles gingerly picks at the pencil nub and pulls it straight out of his arm; it was sticking in a good half—inch. Blood gurgles into the hole, almost dark green in the weird fluorescent light.

"Why don't you call the cops if you think I'm stealing from you," Charles says. He flicks the bloodied pencil piece at her and she recoils.

"Honey, I've got your number," Deonna says. "You call the cops and they're likely to find all sorts of things on you you don't want them to find."

"I didn't say I was going to call the cops. You have no idea what you're talking about," Charles says. "First of all, whatever was in that cat is in Chuck's back left pocket."

Chuck actually looks genuinely surprised. "What? Don't drag me into this," Chuck says. She looks at Chuck for approval and he shrugs. She swipes a couple of fingers into his back left pocket. Nothing.

"You're a real asshole, you know that?" Deonna says.

"What do you mean that the cops're likely to find all sorts of things?" Charles asks, replaying what she just said over. He doesn't like the sound of it.

Deonna smiles. "You have a brown suede jacket in your apartment. The inside chest pocket has a baggie with a tiny little smear of something almost black. You want the cops to find that?"

Charles' jaw drops. "You planted something on me? Why the fuck would you do that?"

"Honey, I planted several things. That's just one. Let's just say you probably don't want any police dogs sniffing around you or your clothes or your car. I call it insurance."

Charles says, "I don't have whatever you think I have. I quit and I'm leaving."

"Say goodbye to your last paycheck," Deonna says.

Charles doesn't answer. He leaves his father and Deonna together, walking toward the front door of the store. He looks at the mirror as he leaves. He realizes that he saw Chuck tuck the baggie into his mirror image pocket. It's in the other pocket.

Charles shrugs and walks out of the front door of Eastern Antiques.

Pale
by Lynn Beighley

Thursday, 6th November 2014

If this was a movie, I'd be complaining about my bridesmaid dress. You'd see me in it, and you'd think, "Hey, she looks kind of hot even if the color is <whatever>." But this is real life. So it should be vile.

And yet, when you see me on the latest episode of YOU TELL ME, the reality show, you'll notice that the color and the dress is perfect. Fits me, and my recently personal−trainerized body, perfectly. The color, ivory, suits my slightly tan skin. My red hair, in extravagant ringlets that cascade over my pale shoulders, well, blah blah blah. It all works. And it damn well better.

I've sold myself out completely. This wedding, my participation in it, pays for my dad's medical crap, the current festivities, and quite a few of my unpaid utility bills. Oh, and much more has been promised if I play along.

So I do. I walk my dad's intended up the aisle. Or rather she drags me along. I am trying (HEY TV PEOPLE, I'M TRYING) to smile and appear happy to be here.

And in front of me, there's Bill Plover. Bill Plover, the rhinoceros of a man who made me a reality show villain when I turned down his wooing on camera. The same Bill who visited my dad every day in the hospital. The Bill who is my dad's best man. Thing is, when I see him, I smile. Because, well, he's okay. In spite of the reality show that pushed him in to asking me out, and proposing, in spite of all of this, I ...

I like Bill. But look, I don't love him. Don't even think this.

If we were, improbably, to enter into a romantic relationship, there'd be a headline. Something like:

"MAN STABBED WITH MANY TOOTHPICKS."

"LOCAL PROGRAMMER FOUND MURDERED WITH HIS OWN FAVORITE ACTION FIGURES."

"REALITY STAR SLAUGHTERED WITH IPAD SHARDS."

Oh, the possibilities are endless. Fortunately, we remain just friends. He looks at me in ways that make me think he wants more, and I glare at him in ways that tell him to fuck off. Nicely. And he does.

But I am not calm when I spot him up the aisle, waiting. Here's the thing: Dad's wedding has been paid for by TV people. And they paid for it so they could film the drama between Bill and me. So I suspect something will happen. A big obnoxious TV thing.

So far, though, nothing. I walk what's—her—name, my dad's new wife, the taxidermist, up the aisle as her maid of honor. Okay.

I step back as I was instructed. The religious ooga booga guy does his thing. And nothing weird happens. America, you fickle viewing audience, you are being kind to me.

So then Dad and the short perky woman kiss.

And then

then

MUSIC. Like someone turned on the Andrea Boccelli. A curvaceous Jessica Rabbit type bursting with twenty—something hawtness steps out in a wedding dress.

I don't know who she is. But she's dressed like a bride, and she's standing next to Bill in front of the preacher.

Okay, it's a double wedding. Bill is marrying this cartoon of a woman. My mouth is open and many happy little gnats are playing chicken with my tonsils. The TV people are getting their money's worth.

I catch myself, just before the big "man and wife" kiss, and close my mouth. I put on whatever semblance of a smile I can.

Hey America, You Tell Me, are you happy? Am I?

A few minutes later, I wander off in search of the open bar.

The Hall of the Mountain King
by Andrew Stancek

Friday, 7th November 2014

Doctor Bilak bounces into the experimentation lab with a smile for the cameras, tosses back his blond mane. "Today is breakthrough time. Results. I guarantee it. I've prepared additional tools. We are about to fly." His steps are lithe, feet crackle with electricity. The general's team and the government grey suits are still watching, third day of the proceedings, from the glassed–in observation deck above. While Bilak is the last resort, the urgency and hope remain high. They tap their fingers and stare while Colonel Brusk reminds them to erase from their collective consciousness yesterday's unfortunate accident.

"Adam's mother had a heart valve prolapse," Brusk says. "A healthy woman of her age should have absorbed much greater voltage. Collateral damage, that's all. Adam watching her convulsions and cardiac arrest might have induced his cooperation. It could have been fortuitous, but unfortunately our subject remains obstinate. In Bolivia, captured *cocaleros* are routinely made to watch the rapes of their mothers during interrogation. And Stalin of course. No need to belabour the point. Accidents happen and Congressional medals would have been awarded if as a result Crowboy had revealed his secret. We'll leave it now to good Doctor Bilak and his specialization."

Bilak floats in the limelight, gloats in the attention. After a career shrouded in obscurity, labouring without recognition in spite of spectacular results, he feels on the verge of receiving his due. His comments are more for his legacy than for the spectators.

"Professor Holzlohner in Dachau performed crucial studies with ice water. His subjects expired after five hours. Such a result would be counterproductive to our research and accordingly this specimen is being removed from the tank after a mere three hours." Bilak watches a burly assistant hoist the grey child's body by the shoulders, then another lifts the legs, and places it on the table. He paces, right hand moves to a nonexistent cigarette in his mouth; he looks up, grimaces, then modulates his voice into paternal concern and kindness. "Adam, any time you'd like to share." He steps back, scrunches his eyes, fingers his hair, taps a foot, stares at the face of the oversize clock on the wall. The second hand moves smoothly through one rotation, a second and a third. Not a sound is heard. Neither the eyes nor the mouth open.

"A potentially fruitful avenue of research is rewarming. Some of Holzlohner's subjects were thrown into boiling water but frequently death resulted. Adam, do you think boiling water might help you speak?"

Bilak stares at the clock again, three, four, five rotations. No one in the observation deck above moves. Then he waves his arms like a conductor bringing in the vocalists in the Ninth. "The risks, all considered, are too high. As eager as I am to study such illuminating data, we'll forego the boiling water. Eppinger, another great mind, concerned himself with seawater. Our subject has been unable to receive nutrients in conventional ways, in order to increase receptiveness to suggestions. We have been hydrating intravenously but I propose to introduce seawater instead. Adam, does that jog your memory at all? Care to contribute?"

Bilak stares at the clockface. Even though the lab is freezing, beads of sweat appear on his forehead and he brushes at them with his left hand. His smile is alarming. "Our volunteer has given his informed consent to a continuation of our studies," he proclaims. His oversized eyes shine and he cocks his head as if to hear a sound no other ear has heard, to see what no other eye has seen. His hand stretches out, long fingers splayed and a white–coated assistant hands him a beaker. "Plain sea water," Bilak says. "Salinity of thirty–five parts per thousand, chlorine, sodium, sulfur, magnesium, calcium, potassium. Himmler was particularly interested in the research. Two research strands are here combined. Only fitting that a subject who himself had previously explored new realms should be under study. We will introduce the seawater into the intravenous. While we await its effects on memory stimulation, we will prepare the electrodes for the study of the cerebellum."

All eyes are fixed on Adam. Like spectators of an execution, they are gripped, willing a breakthrough.

Adam howls. His first sound since the beginning of the performance is high–pitched and inhuman. His back spasms. The body lurches sideways, back, frontwards, violent *grand mal* seizures as legs thrash and head repeatedly bangs against the tub. Fingers clench, wring, arch. The grey suits exchange glances. The Namer speaks into the microphone next to him. His deep voice echoes through the chamber.

"Stop, Bilak. Abort the experiments. We're done. He won't speak."

Bilak reaches out, the hand gripping the electrodes, then looks up to object, lowers his arm, teeters. The words are a blow he cannot bear. The voice from above says, "Release him." Two assistants place Adam on a gurney, cover him with a sheet. Adam shudders once, twice, takes a rattling breath.

The body lifts off the gurney. It is supine, as if still lying on a flat surface. It rises majestically, white face and white sheet, floats to the viewing area, rigid and weightless. Adam's eyes remain closed as the body propels around the expanse of the lab. This flight is nothing like those seen earlier. On his back, eyes closed, Adam circles, circles, circles. After an eternity, the body perches back onto the gurney, and Adam exhales.

An Eighth of Happiness
by Rachel Ambrose

Saturday, 8th November 2014

"There's a man in my bed!" I whisper–shout to Isa as we make coffee together this morning. She scoops the grounds, I fill the coffee–maker up with water. "A real man!"

"As opposed to those fake men you bring home all the time?" she replies, raising an eyebrow. "And … we're whispering so we don't wake him up, am I right?"

"Yes!" I reply, still whisper–shouting. "I met him at the collaboration last night and he was really nice and really cute so he kind of … followed me home."

"Is he a dog?" asks Isa, a smile twitching the corners of her mouth as she reaches for the cereal. "Tell me he's at least housetrained."

I roll my eyes at her. "His name's Finn, and I'm sure he is." Finn's a hell of a lot of other things, too, but I figure she doesn't need that much information before breakfast.

Just like clockwork, the smell of coffee and toast brings a rumpled Finn out of bed. His long dirty–blond hair hangs in his face, but he's at least put on his blue button down shirt from last night and his jeans. "Hi there," he says, surveying the kitchen counter. "Coffee? Please?" He stares at the pot thirstily, his brown eyes almost liquid.

45

"Sure," says Isa, pouring him a mug and handing it to him. "I'm Isa, by the way, Claire's roommate."

"I know you from the restaurant," says Finn between slurps. "I deliver your fish on the weekends, remember?"

"Oh!" says Isa, her hand flying to her throat. "I'm sorry, I didn't recognize you —"

"Without the Bellington logo on my t—shirt, I know," Finn replies. "Bellington Fisheries, for the best catch this side of your barstool." He grins rakishly at me and I pour milk in my cereal bowl to distract myself from the feeling that all my clothes have suddenly slithered off my body.

I didn't mean to bring him back home, I really didn't. But we started walking and talking after a few plastic cups of cheap pinot grigio at the restaurant and eventually we walked and talked our way onto a moonlit bridge, which led to making out, which led to more walking, which led here. And I have to say that Finn (no last name yet) was a pretty damn good catch. Kind and considerate in the sack, which led to me being even more, ah, considerate than I usually am, which led to more generosity on his part and … yeah, let's just say it was a regular Kumbaya circle of awesome sexy times in my bed last night.

We all sit on the living room floor with our Frosted Flakes bowls watching the Today Show. "I can't believe I never got your number," he says, taking a pen and tiny notebook out of his pocket with a flourish. As we leave, he kisses me with abandon, and I try not to wiggle all the way to work. I still don't know his last name, but he's going to call me tonight! Come on, fun Saturday night out! It'll be a wonderful reward for having to pull extra hours at the gallery on a weekend.

Well, after a day of furious Finn—texting under my desk (for stealth purposes), I not only know his last name (which is Barrows), I know his shoe size, his address and his favorite color. I sidestep Frederico's invitation for dinner with his family by saying I've already got other plans, and immediately meet up with Finn at a Greek restaurant nearby. He, of course, orders the lamb gyro and I order a pita pocket with pork, and before you know it, we're making eyes at each other again across the blue marble table. We finish our food quickly, get baklava to go, and head back to his place, which is gorgeously messy (just like my room!) and features a skinny white cat named Dorado, and we light candles, sit on the floor and feed each other baklava, our fingers sliding across each other's tongues. I'm practically naming our children right then and there.

And then the door opens and this fantastic looking lady with honey—colored hair, purple glasses and tattoos up her arms walks in the door, and he says, "Pandora, this is Claire! Claire, this is Pandora, my wife," just as thrilled as can be.

"Your ... wife?" I splutter. "You want to run that by me again one more time?"

"We're polyamorous," he explains as she dives in for a bear hug and he kisses her on the neck. "I thought it would be a great time for everyone to meet and learn a bit about each other."

I slowly look between them, and I think about it for a few seconds. The idea of saying, 'well, sure, that sounds like fun,' occurs to me, but then it also occurs to me that this is not going to work in a million years. "I'm sorry," I say, shaking my head. "I just have no intention of being anybody's third."

I slowly pull myself together and give Pandora a hug. She smells like lavender and cinnamon, and I so wish we could be friends, because some of her tattoos are actually rad. I kiss Finn on the cheek and apologize again, and he smiles a little sadly and says, "It's better to know who you are than to try to be someone you're not," and Dorado gives a little mew as I'm walking out the door. Somehow, though, I know it's going to be okay.

I call Isa on my way home. "Why do the strangest things happen to me?"

47

Till Death Do Us Party
by Gill Hoffs

Sunday, 9th November 2014

Tonight I'm Shirley, and Shirley is cute.

I've seen the photos. She's what my dad would call a doll.

Tom was a lucky guy; knowing her, marrying her, hearing her halting "Yes …" first while on bended knee then again a few weeks later at the altar in Vegas. He tells me all this repeatedly in his kitchen, leaning against the edge of the crumb–freckled worktop while his eyes drink me in through thick smudgy specs. His fingers are fiddling with his wedding band, somehow turning it round his pudgy digit without dislodging the mug of cold tea in his hand. From the pictures on the fridge, I reckon he's gained four stone since her death, easy, poking doughnuts in his mouth to distract him from the absence of kisses, to fill him with the taste of something other than bitter loss. To disguise the tingling awareness of where her lips have been. He sighs and I can smell cinnamon and powdered sugar on his breath. The Krispy Kreme boxes are piled high in the hall.

"Her wardrobe is as she left it, behind the mirrored door in the main bedroom. Top of the stairs, door on the right. I think she'd have chosen something red for tonight. She liked to dance with me to that Chris de Burgh song."

"Of course." I place my glass of water beside the crowded sink. "Do you want to join me upstairs? I'm a quick dresser and perhaps I could help you relax a little before the party?"

He freezes in place as I move towards him, fingers still, nailbeds pale as he pinches his ring. I smile and change direction as if this was always my intended route, walking past him to the stairs where his feet alone have left clear patches on the faded sage carpet, a thick layer of lilac dust covering the rest.

I'm halfway up the stairs, glad of my heels, of something keeping my feet away from all this, when he calls up,

"I know it needs a clean. I know she'd hate it, me living like this. But I read somewhere that dust is mostly human skin and I can't bear to lose any more of her. Not yet. Not to a vacuum cleaner and bleach."

I pause, turn my head enough so he can see I'm not *too* disgusted, and nod my understanding, before continuing my journey up. I don't look in the bathroom, but keep my eyes turned away from the open door, and instead walk into a comfortable shrine to Shirley.

Her perfume is one I sometimes spritz my neck with when wandering through the women's section in the fancier department stores, a light lemony pick—me—up with a classy bottle and three—figure price tag. Her eye—shadows have deep wells in the centre of each shade and are lying open, fluffed with dust, and her blusher brush stands askew in a chipped mug emblazoned with a photo of Shirley posing with a bow and arrow, Tom standing with an apple on his head behind her, and the legend 'My Mrs Never Misses!' in red.

There's a sleeping bag on the bed, spread next to several long dark hairs adorning the dent in her pillow and the thrown back covers of a long—gone hasty morning. I don't know how she died but I gather neither of them was expecting it. For once I have no smile for my reflection as I open the mirrored wardrobe door.

§

"You make *such* an adorable couple — tell me you're planning kids!" Tom's aunt is sweet but nosy, and I let him field her questions with a charming "Now c'mon, don't be rushing us, Jeanette," his arm warm round my shoulders and particularly welcome on this cold November night. He must look like a typical protective husband, guiding his shy spouse round the room at his grandfather's 90th, but I know I'm really his shield, his safety blanket, the prop needed to buy him some time so he doesn't have to admit to the world that she's gone, his Shirley's gone, and life is now a deep dark cave with only the taste of cake in it.

After two hours, three drinks, and four dances with male relatives while Tom fiddles with his wedding ring and twitches a smile in the general direction of his grandpa, we've done our duty and can go without tuts or frowns or any ill feeling. I accept kisses on the cheek and a pat on the bum from one randy relation with the same shy smile Shirley has on display on the fridge at Tom's — 'our' — home, then we're out into the sleet, skidding on the pavement a little as we walk to the car. The orange glow of the streetlights makes ghostly pumpkins of our breath, and you could hang paintings from my nipples. It's bloody freezing but Tom takes the edge off the worst of it, holding me close, and now we're away from the fug of perfume and deodorant (and cannabis on at least two of his nephews), I can smell the whisky on his breath.

When we get to his car we embrace and he shudders. Not desire, not cold, just plain raw *need* of another human being. Of Shirley. He leans his weight on me, pressing my body against the car, the damp seeping through her dress and chilling my back and bum. I hear him inhale long and hard, sucking in the scent of her perfume.

I say, "It went alright, don't you think? Your family seem really lovely."

And he looks at me like I'm speaking in tongues.

I squirm an arm free of his bulk and reach up, remove his spectacles from his face, and see his eyes blink, now totally out of focus. I smile at him, tilting my head to the right as his wife did in photographs, and think of how to tactfully confiscate his car keys so I can drive us the hundred miles or so 'home'. The whisky is sour on his lips as he kisses me, gently, and I don't say another word as I act the good girl and let the alcohol and optical fuzziness bring back his Shirley. Just for a few minutes, just for tonight.

Pus
by Susan Tepper

Monday, 10th November 2014

The thing about holidays is that they're a drag, Pedersen is thinking. In fact he can't remember a single holiday he ever enjoyed. Plus when there are holidays, the little kiddies, his little darlings, are off from school. It doesn't give him much to do. No point cruising the schoolyard to watch a bunch of squirrels hiding their nuts. "He—haw!"

His shout startles the white rat Swoon who dashes into the rat hole in the baseboard. "Hey you stink—face rat get out here!"

Rats, he discovered, living with one, are single—minded the way cats operate. If he had to choose between coming back in the next life as a cat or a dog (or a rat) he would choose rat. Hands down. Pedersen could see himself as an urban rat slinking along the ceiling pipes in restaurant kitchens once they've gone dark. Scouting out interesting morsels left behind by sloppy clean—up staff. A rat's life is a good life, he's thinking, scratching his leg.

That last kid — the one he picked up at the park — that kid was small but older than he looked. He bit Pedersen in his struggle to escape. The bite mark swelled his calf. It's itchy now and still has pus drainage.

Pedersen squeezes out the pus into a rag. He sniffs it. Pus smells bad. Strong yellow pus. He wipes the bite wound.

"Sweet," he says. The kid was sweet in his fury to escape. That kind of strength isn't lost on him. He respects that boy so much. Todd. He never got the last name. Didn't want it. This way no one can call him out on a missing boy named Todd. It's all a big mystery and will remain a mystery, as far as he is concerned.

He wonders how long the pus will continue to flow? Thinking of it as a putrid yellow river polluted by the corporations who let sewage in. A documentary on TV showed a big pipe with rushing brown fluid going into the Tennessee River. Kids swim in that river. Pedersen thinks about driving down to Tennessee to join the river protest. It could be a holiday type of thing to do. He isn't planning on buying a turkey and no one has invited him for a Thanksgiving feast.

He'll mull it over. The kid, Todd, had these long sweeping eyelashes that stuck together when he cried to be set free.

Careless
by Jessica McHugh

Tuesday, 11th November 2014

"Are you sure you don't want a drink? Most people who come here on Tuesday night have some troubles to drown."

Edward McKenzie swirls his cranberry juice as he lifts his eyes to the swarthy bartender.

"No thanks. Alcohol doesn't fix anyone's problems."

"You got a better cure?"

Tapping his pink press—on nails against the silver filigree crucifix hanging from his neck, Edward smiles.

The bartender dries a tumbler and drapes the towel over his shoulder. "Ah, so you're one of those, huh?"

"A big one," Father McKenzie says. "But I'm not looking to get rid of my problems or discuss religion today. I have bigger plans."

His eyebrows lifting, the bartender leans on his hand and trills. "Like what?"

"Like asking you on a date, Mario."

The bartender straightens his spine. When Edward's cheeks redden, he covers his face. "I'm sorry, I didn't mean to be so forward. It's something new I'm trying. Plus ..." Edward bites his lip and lowers his hands so he can meet Mario's gaze. "... I knew if I found someone like you, someone who could accept me, I had to jump."

Mario chuckles. "Did you just say you want to jump me?"

"I — no, I just ..." Edward fans his face with a bar napkin. "I'm sorry, I think I've made a mistake."

A smile spreads across Mario's face, and he lays his hand on Edward's.

"I've seen you here before. You asked Tricia about me, didn't you? About the people I date."

Edward nods, blushing harder.

"I thought you looked familiar. But I could've sworn you were a redhead."

Edward combs the bangs of his blonde wig over his eyes. "I was that night."

"But that was weeks ago," Mario says. "You didn't get cold feet about asking me out, did you? I know I'm cute, but I'm not *that* cute."

"Don't sell yourself short," Edward replies. "But no, it wasn't that. There was an incident back home. A man I know — his wife caught him."

"With you?"

"I didn't instigate it, but yes, she saw something that happened between us." An amused smile blooms on his lips. "It's funny, I thought things would get worse after that. I thought Charlie would lie, that he'd drag me down with him. But he didn't. He didn't involve me in his confession — which is strange, considering ..."

Mario's eyebrows scrunch, but his eyes brighten as he urges Edward on with a nod. As agitated as Edward had been by the situation, Mario's interest calms him. He exhales, and his shoulders relax as he leans forward.

"The point is, I decided not to press my luck. Like it or not, I had to cool off on being ... me, I guess."

"But you're not cooled off anymore," Mario says, grinning. "You're red hot."

Edward rubs the back of his neck. "Ice blonde, actually."

As Mario chuckles, Edward's purse vibrates. He groans as he fumbles with his phone, pulling it out of his purse and squinting at the screen. Still awkward with the new phone, it takes him a few swipes to answer the call. He gives Mario a cutesy wave before facing away on the barstool.

Tossing his hair, he chirps, "Hello?"

"Father Edward, this is Roberta at Shady Grace."

He clears his throat and drops his voice an octave. "Yes, Roberta, how can I help you?"

There's a pause and some light chatter on the other end. When Roberta speaks again, her voice wavers.

"I'm sorry, Father. Your mother has passed away."

Edward blinks. Thanks to the false eyelashes, he's never been so aware of each flutter against his cheeks.

"I was just there for a visit this morning," he whispers.

"I know, I'm sorry."

He taps his knee, his veins running cold as he tries to secure a response through the garbled grief clouding his mind. Shaking, he says, "I'm away in the city right now, but I'll be there as soon as I can. Thank you, Roberta."

Hanging up, Edward sets his phone on the bar and removes his wallet.

"Not leaving, are you?" Mario asks.

"I'm afraid I have to," he says, laying a five—dollar bill next to his phone.

Seeing the screen alight, he realizes the call from Shady Grace is still connected. He swipes the screen, but nothing happens.

"Let me," Mario says. He ends the call with a few nimble swipes but taps the screen a dozen more times before handing the phone back.

"In case you feel like being forward again, you have my number now."

Despite his heartache, Edward doesn't have to force his smile. Looking into the bartender's deep, chocolate eyes, he says, "Thank you."

Kicking off his heels, Edward slumps into his car and looks in the rearview mirror. The fake lashes have left wet, black tracks under his eyes. He peels them off, drops them in the cup holder, and begins the trek across the state to Shady Grace Retirement Home.

Edward gives his face a wipe—down with a towelette in the parking lot and fumbling, pulls a pair of slacks over his pantyhose. He transfers his wallet and keys from his purse to his pockets, and wriggles his blue shift dress up to his waist. It snags on his crucifix as he lifts it over his head, creating a blind struggle until it tears free. Groaning, he tosses it over his shoulder and retrieves a long sleeve polo shirt from the backseat. The sleeves scratch like burlap against his freshly waxed arms; it's strange how unnatural the modest clothing feels, even after decades of wearing vestments. Removing his wig and tousling his mashed hair, he slides on his loafers and strides into Shady Grace.

Roberta's smile is tight as she speeds through her greeting and condolences. Her head bowed, she leads him to Betty McKenzie's room. The overwhelming smell of vodka smacks him across the face the moment she opens the door. A large stain on the carpet appears the culprit.

"She fell. Dropped a bottle. You know how sneaky she was about those things," Roberta says. "If it's too much —"

"No, I'm used to it," Edward says.

"We haven't touched anything else. Her personal effects are here for you to sort through, with three boxes. One for donations, one for things you'd like to keep, and one for items you'd like buried with Betty, God rest her soul." She squeezes his hand. "I'm sorry for your loss."

In the consolation, Edward notices Roberta's back stiffen. Still holding his hand, she gawks at the painted fingernails before casting him a baffled look.

Burying his hands in his pockets, Edward says, "Thank you for everything, Roberta. I'd like to be alone now."

She nods and shuffles down the hall as Edward shuts the door. The vodka smells thicker now. He opens a window and inhales the night breeze. Then, sidestepping the carpet stain, he empties Betty McKenzie's dresser drawers onto the bed beside the boxes.

There's nothing he wants to keep. He separates the clothes into the donation box, and scoops up liquor-stained photos to discard. But before dropping them in the trash, Edward notices a glimmer in the stack. Twirling his finger around the golden chain, he unspools it from the falling photos.

His grandmother's crucifix rests on his palm as perfectly as it always did. It even feels warm. As Edwards closes his hand around it, familiar fingers close on his shoulder.

His face flushes with a smile as he spins and embraces Grandma Eleanor. It's seemed an eternity since he inhaled the scent of her Duska powder, and he could easily lose another eternity to that comfort.

When she takes his hands, her body tenses like Nurse Roberta's had. *Oh Edward, your nails. After what happened with Charlie Kitner, why are you being so careless?*

"Because I don't care anymore, Eleanor. I'm actually a little disappointed Mr. Kitner didn't expose the truth about me. Now I have to do it myself." He sighs, then chuckles. "And for the first time, I believe I can. I believe this is who God wants me to be — whole, happy, and unafraid of a truthful future."

He clutches her crucifix so tight it stabs his skin.

It's yours again. Just like it always should've been. I never wanted your mother to have it.

Edward breaks away. His face crinkled by sorrow, he says, "Which is why she probably needed it. Even now."

With a nod and a beaming smile, Grandma Eleanor embraces Edward once more, kisses his cheek, and urges him toward the bed. He lowers the crucifix into the burial box and swallows hard as he closes the lid.

Illuminated by a new glory, Edward crosses through the empty room. He opens the door, and the antiseptic hallway flushes out the last waves of his mother's alcohol.

Passing by the nurses' station, he raps his tapered nails on the counter. "Everything's organized in the room, Roberta. Thank you. I'll be in touch."

Staring at the garish red fingers, Roberta's brow wrinkles.

"Is something wrong?" he asks her.

She lifts her eyes to him, her mouth agape. Edward offers a smile and touches her cheek warmly as he says, "The answer you're looking for is 'no'."

As he exits Shady Grace, he could swear he already hears the rumor mill grinding.

Bedside Manners
by Shane Simmons

Wednesday, 12th November 2014

W e sit at Uncle John's bed, waiting. Waiting on a doctor, waiting on a nurse, waiting on a sign. Aunt Patricia strokes his hand gently. I look around the ward. There's a man opposite, dangling half his body off the side of his bed. I wonder if I should call someone. The television in the corner is stuck on a news channel and despite the time we've sat here, I have not a clue what is happening in the outside world.

"I'm going to go get something from the shop, do you want anything? Cup of tea?"

She shakes her head, but I don't pay her response too much heed. I'll bring her back a cuppa and a sandwich.

I wander off through the maze of corridors, all painted matching beige and white.

In the hospital's ground floor café I look over the drinks list.

"Large latte please, but can you do an extra shot with that?" The barista nods. He's not too harsh on the eyes.

"Course we can, what's the point of a café that won't sell you extra caffeine?" He smiles and turns back to his rumbling machine. I don't usually pay attention to blonds but my lolling against the counter comes from being knackered as well as half–

arsed flirtatiousness. But I'm too busy rubbing my eyes to *fully* appreciate the scenery.

I take my coffee (and a slyly purchased blueberry and oat muffin) to a table near the window. Hanging from the ceiling is yet another television with a perpetual rolling ticker tape relaying misery and doom. Every corner you take in this place there's a screen, a reminder that you or your loved ones may not be in the best of shape, but hey, the whole world's going to pot so man up because nothing you're going through is *that* bad. It's a cunning ploy.

This coffee's a tad bitter and a little too strong. But I did ask for that extra shot.

I can't tell Aunt Patricia the news. No, not the news on the screen. Other news, which at this moment in time is just not that important. Uncle John's had a stroke. They've kept him sedated while they investigate. Why am I even thinking about the content of yesterday's phone call?

But this news, it can't help but pop into my mind at the most inopportune moments. I'm not entirely sure what to make of it. It hasn't had the chance to sink in. And I want to talk to someone about it. Sandra's off the list. We haven't talked since we got back from Amsterdam and she had gained some sort of recall of what had happened. *I fink its best we dont talk 4 a bit* said her text. Aunt Patricia is understandably preoccupied. It's not important, not in the grand scale, yet I can't help feeling torn between the here and now, and what, according to that call yesterday, could be in store for me.

I stare out of the window at the smokers gathered by the hospital entrance, one leaning on the stand carrying the drip she's attached to. The caffeine hasn't hit my bloodstream yet, but an unexpected tap on my shoulder brings me out of my daze.

"Sorry, is this yours? A customer found it on the counter." I look at the phone in the palm of his hand and realise it is mine. "I think there may be a missed call on it, the screen was flashing when she noticed it." The blond bloke hands it over, smiles and walks away.

I open the call log. It was Aunt Patricia, two minutes ago. At that moment the screen lights up and it whirs in my palm.

"He's coming around, he's mumbled some words!" Her teary sighs are a mixture of both elation and exhaustion.

"I'll be two minutes aunty, I'm just in the café downstairs."

Quick−stepping past the counter I brake and take a few skips backwards. I wave my phone at the blond guy. "Thanks."

"No problem," he smiles, "you've perked up, good news I hope?"

"Yeah." I wonder if I should fill him in, but in this place he probably endures the traumatic stories of many a dull stranger. I thumb in the direction of the exit. "Best get going."

"No problem. Maybe see you in here again sometime," he calls as I speed off.

Dashing down the corridor, I follow the arrows on the walls back to the lift to take me up to the fifth floor.

There at his bedside, a nurse leans over Uncle John, and Aunt Patricia stands back as a pen light is shone into his eyes. The moment she sees me she grabs and grasps my hand. "He asked for a cup of tea!"

I look down at him and between blinks his bleary eyes focus on the two of us.

"They're getting him some tea and toast." She lets go of my hand and stepping forward, smooths the hair on his head. "They'll be here soon, don't worry, love."

Bearing witness to the relief beaming from Aunt Patricia's face, I know this moment eclipses any news I may have.

Postcards
by Michelle Elvy

Thursday, 13th November 2014

T he waitress — *Jen*, as her tag announces with a Florida sunshine smiley face — brings a refill of coffee and a large breakfast plate. She tried to bring a side of grits — *breakfast of champions*, she said — but Stevie has not grown accustomed to this southern mainstay, so he has gently refused the generous offer made by the insistent and happy Jen. He finds himself grinning stupidly at the two eggs on the plate, as if Jen's name tag has some kind of commanding power over him. *Eat and be merry. Smile at your eggs, boy.* And why shouldn't he? It's an agreeable breakfast platter. The bacon rests crinkly on the side, the toast is brown and buttery, the eggs are cooked perfectly, golden yellow with just enough ooze when the fork breaks their surface ever so gently with a soft *pop*.

When the plates are cleared, Stevie asks for a refill and pulls the map and postcards from his backpack. The map shows an overview from Florida to Panama. Places that, up to today, have been exotic names on a page. Now they are within reach, and he's thinking even more about what's over the horizon. The Caribbean … Central America … Panama … Too many unknowns to count. And yet, every time he thinks about it, every time he asks himself whether he should go, the answer rumbles in his chest: *yes.*

For now, he turns his attention to the five postcards on the table: an alligator, some tropical fish, a beach, Cape Canaveral and a big yellow sun: *Greetings from the Sunshine State.* Missives for home.

Home. The Chesapeake. Mile after low mile of farms, sandy shores and grassy marshland. Corn and sorghum. Mosquitoes and fireflies. Assateague and Chincoteague. Baltimore and Washington. Places that make sense to him. Meaning and memories.

And people. Lucky and Manny. Ellie and Sylvie.

All his life contained in one brackish bay.

And now he's travelled nearly 1000 miles to get someplace else. And, despite overflowing with smiling, suntanned people, too many of them orange like the fruits that grow on their famous trees, Florida feels just about right.

"Where you from, sugar?" Jen drops off more creamer for the coffee.

"Um, Maryland."

"You not in school?"

"No. Taking some time off. Sailed down here with my uncle."

"Ah: snowbirds. I get it. Maryland that cold in winter?"

"Yes, cold enough."

"Good trip, then? You come down the ICW?"

"Yes, good trip. But no, we went outside." Outside meaning facing the frothy Atlantic rather than cruising down the relative safety of the Intracoastal Waterway. As he says it, Stevie feels the excitement again, something pulling him away. He doesn't say it because it sounds a little corny, but he feels it deep down: how, sailing out of the Chesapeake last month, he felt like Huck Finn, lighting out for new territory.

"You scared out there? On the ocean?"

"No." He's not surprised at the certainty in his voice when he answers this question. Some things scare him, sure – but being out of sight of land is not one of them. No, sailing offshore has turned out to be not at all what he'd imagined. He finds himself at home under the stars at night, and, despite being more alone than ever, he has also experienced the whole process of disconnecting – no iPhone, no television, no Internet – as strangely liberating. Being at sea was easy. Soothing, even. Plus, he adds for Jen's reassurance, they'd left the Chesapeake just in time; he's heard from his parents that winter has struck early this year and snow's on the way.

"Well. You write them postcards, sugar. You write your parents – and be sure to tell them about how good our breakfasts are, now."

Jen winks and sashays back to the counter. Stevie turns to the task at hand. Not a necessity, but a ritual, part of travel etiquette for as long as he can remember: drinking coffee in a diner booth and sending out small notes to the world is part of any travel plan. Something his mother has engrained in him, like marking a map with your existence, one small x at a time. Or, he thinks now, like a piece of the story, a hint at his existence. A flash of a moment in a blink of an eye. Proof that he was here: terra firma. He likes thinking that a postcard could mean more than what he would actually write, that there is more to the story than what fits on the page. He likes that this small excerpt, or hint, will tell a piece of a whole story – and that this one piece is enough.

First on the pile is the perfect postcard for his little brother, who has a telescope in his room and dreams of stars like Stevie dreams of the ocean. One day his brother will get to Cape Canaveral. One day Rob's life will orbit around a comet research center in California and he'll have many such postcards and photographs on his wall. And this one, a vintage photo from NASA's early years, will live in a small frame on his desk.

> Hey —
> Floating on the ocean is like how I imagine
> space. No line between night sky and sea, and
> stars like you can't imagine. Except it's easier
> to breathe.
> Maybe a better option, sky—boy.
> — Sea—boy

Stevie had seen *Gravity* with Rob just before he left. Stevie has always been afraid of space — but he's been a good brother and watched all the space movies with Rob, who gets a rapt look on his face whenever *Apollo 13, The Right Stuff,* even *Aliens* is the topic. Space appeals to Rob in a way that Stevie gets because he's also drawn away from land. But Stevie doesn't even like flying, much less any notion of leaving his own oxygenated atmosphere. He turns the postcard over and looks at the photo again. Flips it back again and adds:

> PS — Must have seen a hundred shooting stars
> out there. Even if I know they aren't stars.
> You'd have loved that.

Next card is for his parents: a beautiful long beach. The kind you write "wish you were here" on the back of. But Stevie doesn't write about the beach.

> Mom and Dad —
> Read *1984* and *Animal Farm* on the trip
> down. Spooky, your 'classics'. Kinda dry. Also
> found Norm's *Playboys*. Not so dry (joke,
> Mom). I guess Orwell makes a strong case for
> me writing you long—hand. I'm going to order

66

key lime pie before we leave. Big Brother, you
got my order?
Miss you.
– Stevie

PS Still don't like grits.

A huge alligator appears next in his pile. Grinning? Maybe.
Just right for Manny.

Hey –
Haven't seen a single gator but I did see a guy
on a crowded boardwalk with a Where's
Waldo suit and a woman with a prosthetic leg
and an orange bikini playing volleyball and
kicking ass. No shit. Your kind of hot.
(Not the Waldo guy.)
– S

He misses Manny. And Lucky. He's spent all year trying to
run away and now he's finally left them both behind. But the
words "wish you were here" resonate more than he'd ever
thought they could. If he were superstitious he'd write
something about Lucky, but instead he keeps to the real world,
to the here–and–now. To the living. He picks up his pen again,
adds:

PS – Don't forget the road trip, fucker.
See you soon.

The Tropical Fish of Florida are for Ellie, who has just
recently started her term as an intern at the Chesapeake Bay
Foundation and is apparently counting fish, or something like
that. She sounds good on the phone. Like she misses him, yeah,
but also like she doesn't. Typical Ellie – he likes that about her.

And he likes that even though he misses her – of course he does – he was grateful when she said, even when he wasn't sure: *Go.*

Suddenly the challenge of fitting what he wants to say in such a small space is no fun. He always has a million things to say to Ellie. But he can't pack a million things here, so he writes:

E –
See you next month. Can't wait.
– S

Finally, he has only one postcard left in the stack. It's the huge yellow sun. It's for Sylvie, Ellie's little sister. A girl whose presence is as strong as any other in his life, even if he's only spent time with her this year. Still, they have buried a pet canary together, eaten mac 'n' cheese off china, made Jello of questionable mixed flavors and colors – not the kind of things you do with just anyone. He looks at the sun and writes:

Sun's coming up like a big bald head, poking
up over the grocery store – and yeah, it's
bigger here. You'll see one day. Love, Stevie

It's only years later that he'll think about that card again, and the Laurie Anderson song, the one always stuck in his head. Something inherited from his dad. Love. Fear. And strange dreams. Just what life is made of.

Jen's back to pour more coffee but Stevie places a hand over his cup and asks for the check.

"That for your girlfriend?" Jen asks.

Stevie shakes his head. "No, her sister. The fish are for her." He flashes the bright reef fish at Jen.

"Ain't they a lucky pair. But you lucky too, sugar. Don't you forget just how lucky you are."

Stevie flinches. Lucky. *Yep*, he thinks. *Lucky me.*

Callie and Company
by Len Kuntz

Friday, 14th November 2014

In Parsons, Kansas, a tiny place whose downtown is two blocks long, I find myself at a bar. Actually it's more of a saloon. Has a real gunslinger feel to it with swinging half doors at the entrance (how do they lock the place up at night?), a long mahogany bar, antlers framed on the walls, and patrons who look like they just left the state penitentiary. One bald guy has a neck tattoo of a dragon. His glum buddy has a worm–colored scar that runs from middle forehead, through an eyebrow and across the cheek. Knife fight, I'm guessing.

When I walked in, all ten or so drinkers turned but when they saw it was me they looked disillusioned, as if they'd been expecting a stripper who was very late for the party.

I took a seat at the bar, feeling a little twitchy. People had probably died in this place, maybe even recently. I was chum for any one of these barrel–headed guys if they got hot around the collar.

I ordered tequila. It reminded me of Mexico and my honeymoon, my wife and I on a private little dinghy manned by a squat native nicknamed Cannibal who would shout "Happy Hour" every sixty minutes, retrieve a bottle, fill a shot glass with tequila and 7 Up, slam it against the boat's roof, and pass the drink to me or my wife. We got so drunk I hallucinated, seeing sharks in the water that weren't there. My new bride became as frisky as I'd ever seen her and when Cannibal docked the boat at a small tropical island, she lured me away and we made love under a tree that kept dropping bombs around us as we went at it, two kids fucking like rabbits while dodging falling coconuts.

My memory is broken up by the arrival of a young lady who takes the stool next to mine, even though there are a dozen others empty.

"You're pretty deep in thought," she says, her voice sounding a little hillbilly.

"I guess so."

"My name's Callie," she tells me. "I was named for the calla lily. You know that flower?"

"Can't say I do."

The bartender, a huge refrigerator of a man whose name is Earl, says, "I thought your Daddy named you after a Cadillac."

"It's Callie, not Caddy. Come on, Earl. Don't give me any grief. It's been a long day already."

"I bet it's been long," Earl says, wriggling his purple tongue.

I hold up my glass to Earl. "Another, please."

Earl scowls, as if I've insulted him, but he gets me a refill anyway.

"Watcha drinking?" Callie asks.

"Tequila."

"Buy me one?"

I don't like how this is going, yet to refuse her would clearly be an insult. "Sure."

"That's so sweet," she says, patting my knee.

When her drink comes, Callie knocks it back and taps the rim and Earl pours her another, which she downs, just like the third one.

"Whoa," I say, though what I want to say is, *I'm not a fucking ATM.*

Callie starts talking a million miles an hour, saying she's had a patch of bad luck lately, she's a Scorpio, she likes dogs and especially puppies, her dad's an asshole, her mom's okay, Callie's self–employed, and would I like a date?

"Date? No, I don't think so."

She leans forward, massaging my thigh while looking down at some massive cleavage then back to me with a grin. "These are real."

"Great. Good for you."

"Want a squeeze?"

"Hey, I don't think –"

She grabs my hand faster than a striking rattlesnake, and when I try to pull it back, she screams.

Now several of the large felons in the room are up and out of their seats.

"He tried to cop a feel," Callie says. "He molested me."

"I did not."

Earl grabs a baseball bat from under the bar as Dragon Neck and his scar–faced buddy lumber over my way.

I put my hands up. "Look, I didn't do anything."

"I saw you," Earl says. "You grabbed her titty and were holding on for dear life."

"I did no such thing."

"Strangers come in here all the time thinking they can treat our women like dogs."

"I was just making some friendly conversation," Callie says "when he lashed out and groped me. It hurt, too."

"Fucking pervert," Dragon Neck says.

Earl stabs my back with the blunt end of the bat. "We don't cotton to sexual deviants in these parts."

I wish I'd been smart enough to bring the gun along with me. I wish I'd never stopped in this ratty shit hole, wish I'd never offered to buy Callie a drink.

"What're we going to do with him?" Scar Face says.

"I say we break a few bones."

"Please," I say.

Dragon Neck's face is only inches from mine. His breath smells awful. He's had sauerkraut for lunch, perhaps fried liver as well.

"Maybe you'd like to buy your way out of this," Earl says, nudging me with the bat.

I get it now, how this was a set–up. Probably happens any time someone from out of state is unfortunate enough to stop in.

Earl rams me with the bat and a sliver pierces through my shirt and flesh.

"Okay," I say. "How much?"

"How much you got?"

"Look," I say, fishing out my wallet, "I'll buy the drinks, plus how about fifty extra?"

"That wouldn't even pay for ten minutes with a good lawyer."

"Come on guys. Let's be reasonable."

Dragon Neck grabs my shirt by the collar and twists until we are almost a pair of Eskimos rubbing noses. My vision goes cross–eyed. Someone else takes the wallet from my hand.

"All right," I say, as if they need permission, "you can have it. Just leave me something for gas money. That's all the cash I have in the world."

Dragon Face grabs me under my armpits, lifts me off the stool, carries me to the door and tosses me quite literally to the curb. Someone steps over me and into the bar, but not before spitting on my forehead first. My wallet is chucked next to my bleeding cheek.

"Stay the fuck out of here," Scar Face says.

I get up slowly, first kneeling then standing up. Walking to the car I remember I have a gun in the glove compartment.

Inside the car I retrieve the pistol, holding it in my lap. With this gun, I could cause some serious shit, get my money back, even rob the place. I've never done anything so bold before and the idea excites me, the image of myself getting retribution and for once in my life being a badass.

But then a police car pulls over two spots ahead of me. An officer gets out with another cop and together they enter the bar. They're likely all in cahoots – cops, Callie, Dragon Neck. Heck, Earl is probably Callie's dad for all I know.

I drive off not feeling hoodwinked so much as feeling like a loser, cowardly like my wife often accused me of being. I watch the sun starting to set in the distance and remember how sudden the sun in Mexico would descend at a certain point in the evening, as if it got bored and decided to dive into the sea. I think about Mexico and my honeymoon, how it felt like life was just starting. I remember watching my wife blow–drying her hair naked in the hotel bathroom, her skin golden brown except for the places her swimsuit had covered. I remember thinking I'm the luckiest guy in the world, it can't get any better than this, and now as I drive off I realize just how right I was.

Eleventh Inning
by Michael Webb

Saturday, 15th November 2014

It has been a long Saturday, shopping and music lessons and soccer and a doctor's appointment putting us at loose ends and on opposite sides of our suburb. Angela's suggestion of a local restaurant for dinner brought enthusiastic responses. We find our way there separately, and after the customary fussing about seating and ordering and bathroom visits, we manage to get dinner into all four of us. The early round of the playoffs is playing on a television in the corner, and I follow it with distant interest. People assume I watch baseball when I'm not playing, but it's often the last thing I want to see when I'm off duty.

We follow our practiced drill, another bathroom trip for each child, then I settle the bill while Angela ushers the kids into the van, dealing with buckling and strapping and driving home to get ready for the bedtime rituals. I am thinking about the waitress' pert little breasts and the blessed 8−minute ride home, alone in the sedan with the windows open, playing Led Zeppelin into the night, when I push open the wooden doors and step outside.

There is a cute, pudgy brunette, the hostess, standing outside, her back pressed against the wall, her face taut and nervous, looking at a couple on a bench who are arguing furiously with one another. The woman on the bench has her head down, gasping for breath through wracking sobs. Her dirty blonde hair shakes as the man, a stocky guy with a round belly, muscular arms, and a crewcut wearing an Arizona Cardinals jersey pulls hard on the woman's arm. She is leaning away from him, and I can see the red streaks on the woman's arms where his fingers have been pulling. I can feel the fear and tension in the air.

"Come on, Alicia," the man says, too loud and drunkenly. "Come on. Enough of this bullshit. Come home. You're mine."

"No, Freddie," she says between sobs, her voice rising to match his. "I'm not yours. I'm not going anywhere with you. Not now. Not ever."

"You've got to come home," he says. "Come on. Cut the shit. People are staring."

"No I don't," the woman says. "I don't have to go anywhere with you. My sister is coming to get me."

"That bitch," the man says. "Fuck her. You're mine."

"You shut up," she says, looking up at him. Her face is almost purple, swollen and puffy with rage. I feel a heat building in my chest, a red swelling of misshapen rage.

He slaps her face with a suddenness that stuns all of us for a moment. She turns her face away from him and cries harder.

"That's the third time he has hit her," the hostess whispers behind me. "I already called the police."

I step towards the guy. I have a couple of inches on him, and I keep myself in shape. My heart pounds. I hate confrontation.

"Why don't you leave her alone," I say, standing up straight and settling my voice into a low register. "She doesn't want to go with you."

He turns at the sound of my voice, frowning.

"Why don't you mind your own fucking business, pal?" he says. He lunges towards me, his hands out to shove me backwards.

My body moves on its own, the shadow boxing of a million pretend punches at the Athletes Performance Center taking over.

I lean back, letting him stumble, then step forward, loading and firing a crisp left hand into his face, right into the cartilage of his nose. It feels exactly like the workouts do, except at the end I feel flesh giving way instead of the snap of canvas. The gorilla groans and falls backwards between two bushes, his face a mess of blood and mucus.

I hear the sound of sirens in the distance. The woman on the bench mouths the words "thank you," at me.

"Get out of here," the hostess says quickly. "He deserved that, but I don't want you to get in trouble."

I think about headlines on ESPN, how the story would get around the world before the truth gets its boots on, as the old saying goes. I think about getting a reputation as trouble, a nameless rumor drifting across the leagues, turning guaranteed contracts into polite refusals of interest, turning a firm career into becoming a baseball vagabond, pitching for rent money in Korea or Japan. I think about the look on Angela's face when I have to tell her that the gravy train has stopped, that the children's museum board will stop returning her phone calls. I think about the snarl on his lip when he looked at that poor girl, sniveling and crying on the bench, and I thank myself for the presence of mind to hit him with my glove hand and not my pitching hand, and I turn and walk to my car.

The Weight of Sadness
by James Claffey

Sunday, 16th November 2014

Weeks of constant drizzle have the Bird in the doldrums. The darkened days of the butt—end of the year might as well be a giant wet blanket as far as he's concerned. Only the other evening he was polishing the brasses on the front door when the streetlight bulb went out, leaving him completely in the dark, the tin of Brasso in one hand and the dirty cloth in the other.

Lonely is where he lives. This bitter place between bereavement and bachelorhood he has inhabited, a refugee from happier times. If he minds his unemployment money he might be able to take the train to Dublin on the weekend of the Feast of the Immaculate Conception and do a little shopping. He loves the city at Christmas, the lights everywhere and the shop windows so well turned—out and jolly. Might be nice if he could go with the French girl, but she's fallen off the face of the earth and won't reappear in his life again.

Even his own street will string links of white bulbs crisscross between the lampposts and make the place feel quite like another place entirely. Isn't it the most wonderful time of the year, as the song goes? Wonderful if you've family to connect with, or children to play Santa Claus for, or a love to buy a special gift for in the jewelry shops that blare holiday music into the street at a fierce rate. Too bad the Bird has such a weight of sadness crippling him and causing him little joy in his life since he spotted Melodie with her boyfriend.

When his parents were alive they'd have a big crowd in for drinks on Christmas Eve, before Mass, and afterwards presents would be opened in the sitting room before bed. No tree this year, he thinks, preferring to leave the room alone and try to forget all about the season that's in it. As it stands, with the town decked out for the holidays and little chance of his finding anyone to spend this time of year with, the Bird decides to remain desperately lonely and amuse himself with a bit of fishing and a few long walks in the countryside to catch sight of the winter creatures as they battle the elements and try to stay out of harm's way and the hunters' dogs.

In the aftermath of his fried breakfast the Bird makes a trip to the butcher's shop to replenish the bacon and sausage supplies. Behind the counter, red−faced Bartholomew Glynn is cleaving lamb chops from the carcass. The sharpness of the blade leaves a ringing in the tiled interior of the shop and the Bird inhales the scent of meat mingled with blood and sawdust.

"Go on, Bird," Glynn says, wiping his hands on the blue−striped apron. "What'll you have?"

"A pound−and−a−half each of rashers and sausages, thanks."

"Streaky bacon all right?" Glynn drops a slap of rashers on the scales and adds one more strip to even the balance.

"Game ball," the Bird says. He slips both packages in his overcoat pocket and slides a tenner across the glass countertop.

"Any plans for the Christmas?" Glynn asks. He drops the change in the Bird's waiting hand.

"Not a bit. With the parents dead and gone I'll likely stay close to home and heat up a bit of stew."

"God rest them. Didn't they go fast, now that I recall?"

The Bird winces and mutters a reply before turning on his heel and leaving before he can be drawn into any more reminiscences of his poor Mammy and Daddy. Maybe a trip out to the cemetery to put some flowers on the grave? Sure, there'll be no one there on a Christmas afternoon. They'll all be inside watching 'The Sound of Music' or some other bloody nonsense. Desperate lonely, he thinks. Desperate lonely, and awful to have not a soul to spend the time with over the Christmas. He pictures Melodie, all dolled up for the day, heels and lipstick and fresh−scented perfume. He should have held on to her when he had the chance and not allowed her to run like a frightened animal away from him.

Isn't he the fool for not pursuing her, and now her with the eejit from the band? In the door of the house he goes, stopping to put the meat in the fridge. Upstairs something thuds and he shivers a little. "Ah, Mammy, I hope that's not you tormenting me again." He slips along the narrow hall and up the stairs and into the bedroom. Nothing seems out of place, only the window a quarter open to let some air in to the room. With his desperate body odor and unwillingness to bathe more than twice a month lately, the Bird can barely stand his own pong. "Are you here, Mammy?" he asks.

Silence.   Silence.   Silence.

A quiet lie−down, he thinks. His overcoat as blanket, the Bird shuts his eyes and slips off into dreams. The scent of cooked turkey and fresh plum pudding fills the air and voices raised, interspersed with the small pop of crackers being pulled. Happier days. Downstairs he treads, loosing his belt expectantly for the big meal that awaits him. In the dining room the Mammy and Daddy are eating and drinking with abandon and wave him over, beckoning him to sit in his place. He sits and takes a large mouthful of wine. The soft French accent of Melodie asking him, "Bird, do you like the stuffing on the side of your plate?" Smile. Her gentleness. The warmth spreading about his heart a layer of insulation against the loneliness. How lucky he is to be in love, to have the parents he does, and to be content in all his being.

He pulls the overcoat tight, the cold air seeping in the window. Melodie's lips press against his cheek and she whispers, *"Joyeux Nöel,* Bird. *Joyeux Nöel!"* In happy dreams the Bird leaves the worries of the world behind and is taken away to a place where the unfairness of his life evaporates into vapor.

Live with That
by Gwendolyn Joyce Mintz

Monday, 17th November 2014

He just has to move the boxes out onto the porch for Goodwill to pick up later in the week. Then Aaron will go get Phil for the meeting.

Back in the living room, he stands before his posted 'to do' list. He makes a line through an item and then peels the paper from the wall.

He sighs with content.

All done, save for one and he could live with that.

Or die with it, as the case may be.

Stand Up
by Stephen V. Ramey

Tuesday, 18th November 2014

The clouds are heavy today. We haven't had a real snow yet, but the weathercasters are hopeful. Not enough drama in their lives, I guess.

We're cruising down Jefferson in our beat–up pickup truck. I've seen this street a thousand times, but it looks different today, probably because Anne is at the wheel. She offered to drive me to my oncology appointment on her way to work. She's been kind since my return, more than kind. Loving. The more I think about it, the more it's clear that she always was loving; it was my perspective that changed us. Resentment at the world, maybe. There's no grudge like a disappointed idealist's grudge.

"Do you need me to pick you up, after?" she says with a sideways glance. Her eyes are green. I never actually forgot that, but haven't really paid attention in a while.

"No, it's okay," I say. "Just an office visit. I'll walk back." The doctor is designing a new protocol for us, moving forward. He was stern with me for breaking our last appointment – how long has it been? Three months? Four? – and I thought he might even drop me, but he didn't. *People react in different ways* – this with a sigh as he's studying the latest scan – *I take it you're in now, Stephen, right? I mean all in. This is not going to be easy on you.*

Yes. I think of Mystery dying in my arms, her eyes on me, watching, expecting, the hole in my chest filling with grief.

"All the way."

Anne frowns. "What?"

"Oh, nothing. Just thinking out loud." A white billboard catches my eye. *Stand Up for New Castle* in bold red letters above a silhouette of people joining hands. "That's new, isn't it?"

Anne chuckles. "If you count six months as new." She drops one hand from the steering wheel and squeezes mine. "I swear you wouldn't see the sun if I didn't point it out to you."

I feel a sting of irritation, let it pass. "I've had a lot on my mind, I guess."

"True," Anne says, returning her hand to the wheel. "That's the group I've been volunteering with. We're working to save the Cooper building." She glances. "Your letter helped, you know."

"Letter?"

"The letter to the editor? Remem —"

"Oh, yeah. I just dashed that off." And I did, mostly. That was the day Rose touched my cheek, the day this all began. I probably should wish that day never happened, but I don't.

Anne sighs. "You have such a gift, Stephen, so much passion. If you'd just learn to channel it —"

"I'd be famous." I stare out the side window. "Has it ever occurred to you I don't want to be famous? I just want to be left alone, do my work, leave something meaningful behind."

"Yes, yes, I know. You're the great altruist, you don't seek validation from others — that's *my* flaw. We've had this discussion, I'm not dense."

Heat floods my head. "What are you saying, Anne? That I'm lying to myself, that I don't mean what I say? Well, I —"

"That's not what I'm saying." Anne looks straight ahead, blinking too fast.

"Then what?" I shake my head.

"What I'm suggesting," she says steadily, "is that you can't leave something behind if you were never here."

Everything crashes at once, the sky, my anger, the Stand Up sign; it's all falling around me, shrapnel from an explosion I never dreamed possible. *She's right. Exactly right.*

The truck starts across the downtown bridge. I glimpse the river churning below, deep and green and never ending.

I touch Anne's arm. "I'm sorry. I'm ... I may be dying. I'm scared."

Anne looks at me. For an instant I worry she's going to drive us off the bridge, then I decide it doesn't matter. As long as it's with her. I don't even notice the tears until they're sliding down my cheek.

In my mind, Mystery looks up from my chest, those golden eyes bright with some hidden fire. *It's about time.*

Returns
by Gay Degani

Wednesday, 19th November 2014

Mars slicks back his hair, damp from his shower, checks the thoroughness of his shave in the mirror, straightens his frayed denim shirt. Not bad, he thinks. The best he can do in a place like this. He misses Rita. At least, he misses her house, her hot tub, her bed. He grimaces, shakes his head. Better get going.

He strides out of First Light Mission into the bracing air and turns south. Cars rumble along the parkway, an old Beastie Boys song pounding from someone's radio. Mars lifts his chin. Beneath a cloudless sky, the peaks of distant mountains gleam white. The song he just heard repeats in his head. "You gotta fight for the right to parrrr—tee." He grins. With Thanksgiving just a week away, there should be plenty of work.

"Hey, man. Slow down."

Mars pivots, and waits as a short, solid man trots to catch up.

"Javi," says Mars. "How's that bambino?"

The other man rolls his eyes. "En español es 'bebé'. No sleep. Nada. My wife is, uh, es como un jaguar. Walking, how you say, how you say — when you walk up and down, up and down?"

"You mean, pacing? She's worried?"

"Yes, yes. She worry. She tired. No sleep. No money. No happy."

"Well," says Mar, slapping Javi on the back, "then we'd better get at it."

Three blocks down, a group of laborers mill around in front of the Home Depot, some sitting on a low cinderblock wall, drinking coffee, others smoking, kidding around, a few approaching pick—up trucks as they turn into the parking lot. A couple of guys linger across the street in front of the U—Haul, although a Wednesday in the middle of the month isn't prime moving time. The best jobs come from contractors and do—it—yourselfers, especially if a worker can hang drywall, lay brick, install a laminate floor. Mars can do all these jobs and hopes someone will take him on as a regular, at least through the holidays.

An Escalade slows to the curb and Mars and Javi look up expectantly. The passenger window rolls down and the woman behind the wheel leans across the seat, takes off her sunglasses, and smiles at Mars. "I need someone to remove some wallpaper?"

Mars puts a hand on the window frame, smiles back. He wonders if she's a realtor like Rita or maybe a house flipper.

Javi pipes up, "I can do that. Real good, real fast, real cheap."

She's still eyeing Mars. "Are you real cheap too?" but he backs away, glances at Javi. "This young man's the best you can get and very reasonable for the quality of his work."

Her lips part in surprise, her head tilts, and then she turns to Javi. "How much?"

"Only eight dollars an hour."

"Ten and he's a steal." Mars nods at her, and she nods back.

"Okay, Mr. Ten—Dollars—an—Hour. Hop in." And Javi does just that.

Mars watches the SUV speed away as another car, strapped with an empty trailer, bumps from the U—Haul lot over the curb into the street and up the Home Depot driveway, sending men scrambling.

"What the hell?" hollers Mars. He recognizes the driver, Ian Shane, at the same time Ian Shane recognizes him and Mars jumps out of the way thinking Rita's son plans to run him down. This is the guy he put in the hospital a couple of months ago, whose mother accused Mars of killing that woman down by the creek.

But the car and trailer screech to a stop and Ian starts laughing. "You should see your face. Like I'd try to take you."

"What happened just now?" Mars opens Ian's car door. The laborers bunch up around them.

Ian shrugs. "Saw you when I was getting the trailer, and I wasn't paying attention when I headed this way. Thought you might want some work?"

"What kind of work? Not with your mother."

"She's gone. You wanna help me move?"

"What do you mean, she's gone?"

"Get in and I'll tell you all about it."

Even if this is a trick, Mars knows Ian Shane is no threat. Gus calls him the shiny penny, the mama's boy. Mars says, "You'd better let me drive."

Once they're on their way, Ian says, "She cut me off, you know. Fired me, stopped paying my rent. Took off with some dude to Bali."

"I thought she was going to get rich on the Old Road development."

"Dead in the water. Hey, listen, I'm sorry she gave your name to the police. Sorry I had anything to do with it."

"Hey, the cops thought I did it because someone saw me talking with her. I didn't even know her name, but they pulled me in more than once. Dragged me out of the shelter a couple of weeks ago. They're probably watching me now."

"Why'd they let you go?"

"No proof," Mars gives Ian a hard look, "because I didn't do it."

"Her name was Charmaine Martin," says Ian.

They drive in silence for a while, the empty trailer rattling behind them, until Mars says, "Sorry you got cut when I hit you. I just wanted to hit you."

"It was okay. That was crazy all of us at the hospital in the middle of the night. Your dad seems to be doing alright."

"I guess. I don't see him much."

As Mars turns into the Old Road, he asks, "So where you moving to?"

"In with a friend. He's got a condo downtown."

"What are you gonna do, you know, for money?"

"Real estate. It's what I know. It's what she taught me. I just didn't realize she was such a bitch. Hey, who's that Sybil's talking to in the courtyard?"

Mars, busy thinking he should have come in from the other direction, to park on the same side of the street as the bungalows, glances up to see a group of people turning toward them, shading their eyes. Sybil, who owns the property where Ian Shane is moving from, stands next to a young woman. Another man is with them, and two children, a girl and a boy, chase each other around the adults. Gus German, Mars' father, watches from the front porch of his bungalow.

"That's Jamie," says Mars, pulling to the curb and turning off the engine, "and her kids."

"I thought she'd been, you know, kidnapped – or worse."

"No, not her. She just took off, I guess. She's safe." The break in his voice surprises him.

"That guy's the murdered woman's husband. Name's Sam. He's some kind of doctor."

"I never met him," says Mars. "You ever think he might have done it?"

"Yeah," says Ian. "It's usually the husband."

Nørthærn Lights

by Sally—Anne Macomber

Thursday, 20th November 2014

To: Milton Flaxmill, Red Cow Publishing
Bcc: Leonard Strauss Jr., Red Cow Publishing
From: Trudy Polaris
Date: November 20, 2014 2:06 p.m.
Re: Hilsænær frå Øslø!

Årt hås triümphæd øvær cømmærcæ!

I åm hæræ in Øslø in thæ lææd–üp tø thæ Nøßæl Prizæ–giving cæræmøny, which is ønly 20 dåys åwåy. Øsløviåns åræ væry håppy åßøüt this. (Thæy ønly givæ øüt ønæ øf thæ Nøßæls in Øslø – thæ ræst thæy givæ øüt in Støckhølm (did yøü knøw this?) – sø I åm høping thæ Nøßæl thæy givæ in Øslø is thæ ønæ with my nåmæ øn it.)

Lææving thæ Tyrøl wås væry dråmåtic. I snück øüt in thæ dæåd øf night! I tøøk sævæn gøåts with mæ, høming gøåts tråinæd tø find thæ Swiss Børdær. I læft my hüsßånd å nøtæ ßæsidæ my cømpütær kæyßøård – *Gønæ fishing!* – ånd with thæ sævæn gøåts linkæd tøgæthær øn å løng røpæ, strück øüt før fræædøm! Wæ sång søngs åløng thæ wåy tø kææp øür spirits üp – søngs frøm my müsicål *Silåsj Silåsj Silåsj* – thæ nøtæs ßøüncing øff thæ

90

cliff fåcæs, thæ high nøtæs ålmøst cåüsing åvålånchæs, ånd ßy thæ timæ wæ'd rün øüt øf søngs wæ'd jüst mådæ it tø thæ ßørdær.

Øf coürsæ, it wåsn't thæ ßørdær with Switzærlånd – dæspitæ my tålænt før oriæntæering I coüldn't find Åürørå ßøræålis ånd thæ goåts læd mæ tø Liæchtænstæin instæåd – ßüt crøssing intø næütrål tærritøry, I wås nævær sø glåd tø sææ thæ ßåck øf thæ Tyrølæån tåx håvæn thåt øvær thæ prævioüs æight mønths håd ßæcømæ å tåx prisøn!

I søld thæ goåts tø å tålænt scoüt før sømæ müch–næædæd æürøs øn thæ Liæchtænstæin ßlåck mårkæt ånd cåshing in thåt fræe flight coüpøn frøm ßülgåriå Åir I'væ ßæen kæeping før å råiny dåy, flæw tø Øslø.

Thæ ßülgåriå Åir flight wås tærrißlæ, ßümpy ånd cønfüsing (thæ ßülgåriån I læårnæd whæn I wås thæ Fættå ÅmßåssådrÆss wås thæ wrøng ßülgåriån it türns øüt!) ånd thæ ønly føød åvåilåßlæ øn thæ inflight mænü wås sømæ sæcønd–hånd goülåsh ånd rætsinå–infüsæd håsh ßrøwns. It wås likæ åll my prævioüs livæs cøming ßåck tø håünt mæ!

ßüt nøw I åm hæræ før thæ Nøßæl fæstivitiæs.

It woüld ßæ ønæ øf thæ 10 møst impørtånt highlights øf my lifæ if it wåsn't før thøsæ snæåky Nøßæl Prizæ–giving ßåstårds! I cån find nø mæntiøn øf my nåmæ ør *Nüclæår Fissiøn in Thæ Himålåyås* ør thæ virgin–værsiøn *Nüclæår Fissiøn in Thæ Pyrénéæs* ør ævæn Ræd Cøw Püßlishing ånywhæræ. It's likæ Øslø is dæåd tø üs! Thøsæ Nørwægiåns åræ icy cøøkiæs indæed!

I åm wøndæring if måyßæ nøt håving å Nørwåy trånslåtiøn ræådy før thæ Præss ånd thæ püßlic ånd thæ Nøßæl jüdgæs wås süch å goød idæå. Is sømæthing ßæing dønæ åßoüt thåt? Ånd whåt åßoüt thæ Frænch ånd thæ Itåliån ånd Gærmån ånd Swiss Gærmån ånd Åüstriån–Gærmån ånd Tyrølæån–Åüstriån ånd Spånish ånd Tågåløg ånd Süømi trånslåtiøns tøø? This is thæ stüff thåt's kæåping mæ åwåkæ åt night in my süitæ åt thæ Røyål King Kristiån XVII Høtæl, which I åm chårging tø my Ræd Cøw Püßlishing fütüræ æxpænsæ åccøünt, Miltøn. This is thæ stüff thåt måkæs mæ tøss ånd türn in my swånsdøwn ßæd ånd sænd øüt tø røøm særvicæ før midnight hærring!

(I håvæ ßæææ mæåning tø ßring üp this issüæ øf trånslåtiøns øf thæ ßøøk før sømæ timæ nøw, ånd ålsø ån åüdiø ræcørding ßæcåüsæ I think thæ hård øf hæåring will pårticülårly løvæ my ßøøk.)

My intærnæt cønnæctiøn hæræ åt thæ Røyål King Kristiån XVII Høtæl is rünning øüt sø I åm høping yøü cån wiræ mæ sømæ mønæy før thæ dræss I will ßæ wæåring tø thæ officiål cæræmøny. Thæræ's å løt øf øcæløt øn thæ strææts øf Øslø ånd it's clæårly thæ løøk dü jøür, sø if yøü knøw øf ånyønæ with cønnæctiøns in thæ øcæløt indüstry hæræ in thæ frøzæn nørth, thåt wøüld gø øvær ßig with mæ.

Øf coürsæ, å ræspønsæ frøm yøü wøüld gø øvær ßig with mæ tøø, Miltøn!

Jüst kidding.

Wæll, nøt ræålly kidding.

Ånywåy, gøttå gø!

Yøür fåvøüritæ åüthør ånd minæ,

Trüdy Pølåris

The Retreat
by Mandy Nicol

Friday, 21ˢᵗ November 2014

Mum's being so nice, so solicitous, so unlike herself, that I don't want to force the facts on her. So I thank her for breakfast and say yes, I might stay in bed a little longer.

She thinks Charlie dumped me. She's wrong, it was me who dumped Charlie.

She shuffles out of my room. Persephone pauses in the doorway, sniffs the air, glares at me, then trots off down the hall. I can't see Peregrine, he's probably outside with Anthony. Anthony's been auditing the farm, whatever that means. I asked him if he had to count all the fence posts and he rolled his eyes at me. It stopped him asking me to help.

I shimmy up to a sitting position and rest the plate on my lap. Crispy bacon, boiled egg, toast soldiers. I fold a piece of bacon into my mouth and wonder not so much why I broke up with Charlie, but why I couldn't have waited a bit longer to do it. We were going to Tassie next month on holiday.

But Charlie has been scaring me a lot lately.

It started with babies.

Any kid in a pram or on a television nappy ad got Charlie grinning and winking at me. He was peppering conversation with irrelevant questions like how many children did I want and did I have any names picked out. Last weekend as we walked to his car after seeing a movie he paused a little too long at Bartlett Jewellers' window display. Yesterday he emailed me a dozen photos of houses for sale.

Yesterday I panicked.

I rang and told him it's over.

First he laughed, thinking I was joking. I said it was hardly something I'd joke about and he stopped laughing with a gasp. He kept asking why, even after I explained it five times, so I told him again and there was a long silence. Then he said I was over-reacting. His voice got high and I thought he was going to cry. He offered to slow things down until I caught up with him and I nearly gave in but I didn't. I felt like a bitch. There was another long silence and I started to say I wanted to stay friends but I knew that would be worse than the silence so I stopped. Finally he took a deep breath and thanked me for wasting six months of his life. Then he said he'd still go to Tassie and take his brother with him.

Last night I dreamed of frying pans and Tasmanian Devils.

I pick up the teaspoon and crack open my boiled egg. The yolk's hard and the white is, well, grey.

I shove the plate on the bedside table and wriggle back under the blanket.

Moving on Now
by Margaret Bingel

Saturday, 22nd November 2014

Nora never picks up on the first ring. To discourage telemarketers. She's in the kitchen, five feet away from the wall where she keeps the phone mounted, and lets it ring once. Then before it lets out another shriek, she grabs the receiver and whips it to her ear. And says nothing, breathing into the mouthpiece.

"Mom, it's Ned," says her son on the line, leaning against the counter in his kitchen. "You can say hi, you know."

"Hey Boy," Nora answers, her head tilting to the left, pressing the phone into her shoulder. "What can I do for you?"

Nadia pokes her owner's knees with her nose. Ned looks at his dog and reaches a hand down to pet her.

"Look, Mom, I was thinking." Ned scratches his nails deep into Nadia's furry neck. Nadia pants, wide-mouthed and happy. "As much as I would like to have Thanksgiving with you this year, I'm thinking we should do our own dinners." He holds his breath.

On the other end of the line, a solitary nail on her right hand traces a long-forgotten pencil line on the wall, Ned's last height measurement at seventeen. A small smile breaches the corners of Nora's mouth. "That's fine, Boy," she answers from a faraway place. "I understand."

One minute, the longest minute in their lives, passes between them.

Nora shatters the silence first. "I guess it'll just be me, Rob, and a candlelit turkey dinner." A weird laugh drops out of her voice, nothing forced, just embarrassed.

Nadia flops down at her owner's feet, and Ned bends down to rub her belly. Now Ned's mouth breaks out in a wide grin, thinking about the two most important women in his life: the one who gave him his first life, and the one who gave him a second.

"That's fine, Mom. You and Rob'll have a very nice time together. Nadia and I'll probably go to a friend's house."

Now Nora holds her breath. But she can't hide her wonder, her fingers entwining around the coils of the phone cord. "A friend? Who, may I ask?"

"No one you've met yet, Mom," Ned answers, thinking of Jeffery.

Nora turns her wrist to look at her watch, and frowns. "Ned, I have to get going. I'll have to talk to you some other time."

"Of course, Mom. Goodbye, I love you, I'll talk to you later."

"Love you too, Boy." And then Nora says, "Well, I'm certain we'll both have our own fun times for Thanksgiving."

Some Kind of Important
by Darryl Price

Sunday, 23rd November 2014

Hello, Doc. That's how you can tell it's me or else Bugs Bunny. One of us is always writing to you for answers for the big carrot questions. I guess that makes you some kind of important person in the universe, at least in the universe of me, for which I am grateful. Please don't ever doubt that thankfulness in me. Let me do all the doubting. I'm good at it. I would have made a good doubting Thomas for the Last Supper.

Now down to our current business.

How do I know if I'm still alive? I mean I must have been alive once, granted, because I remember so much of it, but, truly, Doc, how do I tell if you're a much−needed figment of my imagination, or just me spinning in my grave? You could be a ghost from head to toe conjured from out of my loosening mind to have someone to talk with while I'm breaking apart, spreading throughout the cosmos like some kind of foggy stardust. Maybe you're a sparkle on a grain of cosmic debris or something floating there, just out of the corner of my eye, so to speak.

What started me on all this was I can't seem to find any proof of anything anymore. Just because I think I'm here does that mean I'm really actually here? And if I'm not here where am I going? Can I take someone special along with me?

This whole thing really bothers me lately, mostly because I want to know if love is real, or not? I know that's a pretty big, silly question, but it suits the mood I'm in. If love is at least a very real possibility, that tends to make everything else well worth it, doesn't it? Does it not?

I won't go in the opposite direction. I can't. I'm not that person any more. I'm changed. I want to believe in things that are good for you.

I'm scared, Doc. I don't want to lose someone I love again.

Maybe we'd better get right to the letter's private little story and discuss all this deepening shit at a much later time in life: once there was a bright little ghost who was also a philosopher. He constantly argued with the other ghosts that being a ghost was a kind of life. They of course called him a liar and a crazy troublemaker. I only want to be your friend, said the little ghost, but the others didn't like him asking all those hard to answer questions about their natural feelings all the time, so they plotted against him. One night as he was floating through the gloomy forest three larger ghosts jumped on him and held him down. Ghost arms can hold down ghost shoulders, I guess. They splashed an awful smelling purple potion all over his sweet face which instantly disfigured him, but it didn't kill him, well he couldn't be killed, but it didn't make him permanently disappear like a pinched out flame on a candle either as they had been told it would by the witch who sold it to them for some freebie ghost sweat, which is hard to extract under any circumstance. Anyway the three immediately felt quite terrible for what they had done to their innocent friend and began to weep, moan and wail. The little ghost wiped off his wet face on a bunch of moon−lit leaves and just like magic it returned to normal right before everyone's astonished eyes. That witch cheated us, said the first ghost. Yeah, said the second, he's as good as new. The third ghost only continued to moan as if someone had dropped something heavy on his foot by mistake. The four of them became abandoned housemates after that, and still periodically fight over whether being a ghost is being something rather than being nothing.

Thanks for the listening radar ears, Doc. I await your many answers within answers, as they always bring me great relief and set me back on the immediate pathway to heaven.

Neighbor Relations
by Teresa Burns Gunther

Monday, 24th November 2014

Larry

My wife says I'm mad. I've been married to Joyce for twenty–three years; she has a big heart but a blind spot where it concerns the girl next door. I tell her she should be nice to Rachel.

"Why? She's a bitch."

"Nah, just awkward. Did you read the bits I printed out?" Joyce makes a face. "They explain a lot about her. And I just asked them round for turps."

Rachel is odd, but kind; she tries. Like the time she saved Joyce's rabbit, though it was already dead. I never let on that I knew, didn't tell Joyce either, she'd have used it as evidence to build a stronger case. But it means she doesn't know the girl's heart. "I asked them over to thank her boyfriend for his help yesterday, shifted all that timber and soil to the back."

"Boyfriend eh? Must be a fruit loop himself," Joyce says.

§

When the bell rings I squeeze her shoulders and press my forehead to hers. "Now give them a chance, wontcha?"

Rachel hands Joyce a pie in a bakery box. "Berry Cobbler, but it's not homemade."

"Looks a beaut," I say and give Rachel a one–armed hug. Kevin brought a bottle of Shiraz, from the Coonawarra. Nice touch that. Joyce gives him an approving smile. Rachel sees the loom in the corner and her big brown eyes go wide.

"These two are do–it–yourselfers!" she tells Kevin. He nods and grins, he's besotted and I want to hug the bloke for loving this awkward girl. She's a looker, though. Long legged and curved up just right, pretty face.

First glass of wine
Rachel

Joyce is wearing a red dress too, though mine is short and has a belted waist; she doesn't look pleased. Her eyes run me up and down then study her own self. She's round and stumpy to my slim and long, but she laughs and makes a joke. She thanks me for the pie.

Larry's beaming, so proud of Joyce's woven goods: blankets, pillows, and scarves. He says, "My Joyce can make anything beautiful." They're a surprise, colorful with textures that make me want to run my hand over them. I ask if I can touch and Joyce puffs up, *of course* she says and presses her clutched hands between her massive breasts as I tell her how pretty they are. "I'd like to watch how you do it." She gives me a quick demo on her loom and I can see something new, something smart and sparky in her.

Larry leads us out to sit under their twinkle lights. He puts a match to wood in the belly of a Mexican clay stove that snaps and cracks in its belly. It's three days before Thanksgiving but it's warm tonight. I have the view they have of my back porch and kitchen window. I've heard them so many times with friends in their garden, laughing, playing music; now I'm the guest. The only time I was here I was sneaking their dead rabbit I'd washed back into its cage. I thought Stella killed it but she'd just dug it up after it was buried. I wonder what it means that I'm here.

"You have a beautiful garden," I say and I'm hit with a fizz of emotions that threaten to bubble into the open over the round metal table dressed in a hand−woven cloth, a jar of flowers and ferns from their garden sits at its center. "Maybe you could give me some tips." Larry's crook−toothed smile makes me want to ask if Australians are like the English when it comes to orthodontia, but I stop myself − people skills in action. Larry looks over into my yard and practically sings about my concrete slab's potential.

Second glass of wine
Joyce

She brought a pie, for cocktails? – odd that. Store bought, too. Her brows shot up when she gave it to me, nervous? Then her face lit up when I said I love berry cobbler, giving me a snapshot of what she must've looked like as a wee girl. She says she left the whipped cream at home, says she'll go get it.

"Honey," I say, my hand on her arm – she's almost a foot taller. I don't call anyone *Honey*, that's an American thing that annoys me but suddenly I get it. Honey. This tenderness that rises up in front of the words you thought you were going to say. "Honey, it's okay. Cream I have – just look at me." Larry grins like he's won me over to his side, but *she* has. He's been telling me she's one of those borderline autistic types. I always just figured her for rude but he downloaded these articles from the internet for me. Expectin' me to study before drinking with people? But I'm glad he did. I see now what he's been yammering on about. Her dog, Stella, now there's a problem. The creature's vicious. Went after me once.

Her new bloke, Kevin, says Stella's a sweet dog. "But it took her a while …"

"And a few bones," Larry volunteers with a laugh.

Rachel says Stella is just protecting her. That Kevin brought her dog a bone and now he's in. She beams at Kevin and it's sweet, this innocent young love. Larry watches them holding hands with a big grin. Goofy, that's my man. That's what I thought the moment I met him. My mother said, "Bad teeth, bad future," but she never really knew him or the feel of his loving arms. Larry has proved her wrong all the way around. But the dog, I'll keep my distance thank you.

Goodnight
Kevin

I'm keen on this friendship, they're interesting; good people. I think it would be good for Rachel to get to know them. She has no family – unless you count her mother who doesn't know her anymore or that father. The asshole missed her birthday. I wanted to hunt him down and feed him a slice of my furious logic. But Rachel says she doesn't care. She's always so pragmatic. She just said, "That's the father I got." I love her more just for that.

Larry and Joyce stand on their porch, calling goodnight to Rachel and me.

I wrap my arm around Rachel. "So?" I ask.

She says, "It was fun. I think Joyce just needs to get to know Stella. I'll take her over this weekend and surprise her."

Morgana Malone and the Sign of the Boisterous Horse
by Matt Potter

Tuesday, 25th November 2014

"I feel as though I should read it, everybody's talking about it," her voice trills above the hushed crowd. She smiles and the brim of her black straw hat dips over one eye. She must have practiced the move hundreds of times in front of the mirror, it's so perfect, her blonde blunt—cut falling across one side of her face, and draping down across her shoulder on the other, just as her eyes look up. She laughs. Well, neighs almost, shaking her nose and mouth and whinnying. Then she points her toe and hoofs at the carpet.

Perhaps she isn't hoofing at the carpet but her hair is what I *thought* I was getting way back in January when I had mine dyed orange and bobbed. (Which is still half—grown out.) Under her straw hat her mane is sleek and lustrous.

I don't know who she is but then, I don't really know who any of these people milling and chatting and smiling and reminiscing are either.

Turning my gaze to the framed photo of Mr Rubinstein resting on the table beside the condolence book, I raise the teacup to my lips and shift my weight from my left foot to my right, with what I think is a faraway look in my eye. Like I do this every day, this weight–shifting, faraway–looking, standing–beside–the–piano–all–on–my–very–own–looking–slightly–uncomfortable in a room with 200 other people sort of thing.

I drain the cup and place it on the saucer on the polished, upright piano, which unlike the piano Marco Garibaldi uses when he struggles to teach me singing every Saturday afternoon, is completely free of stacks of sheet music.

I can't imagine why anyone would want tinkling piano music playing as the mourners offer their condolences to the family, but then I've never been to a Jewish funeral service before so everything is novel.

"Whoa, sexy glasses," Seth says over my shoulder.

(Actually, everything is novel because with my new glasses, I'm seeing *everything* for the first time in I don't know how long.)

Seth steps around me and I breathe in his treacly cologne as his arms envelop me in a hug. It's nice to know he thinks he can still do this, eight weeks and five days after we broke up. Although "broke up" implies something that, I don't know, maybe it wasn't.

Seth looks at the grey and brown regrowth spreading across my head and says, "You are one seriously foxy woman, Morgana." And now he looks in my eyes. "And your glasses are so (and here he stops as he considers his words) ... *becoming.*"

If I didn't know better I'd think he was joking, but I do know better, and a smile creeps across my face.

"Opi would be very happy you're here," he adds, with just the vaguest, slightest, tugging catch at the end. His eyes are ringed red and the tip of his nose is pink and I look at the high cheekbones on his thin face and short dark hair atop deep brown eyes and I am struck again by how much he looks like Grigor. Even Grigor after his plastic surgery.

And I can't help it, it just flies out of my mouth. "Mr Rubinstein was a wonderful man and he adored you."

Seth smiles, that 1000—watt grin he flashes the moment he first wakes up. "Yeah, well, he was Opi and he was special."

"He was, he always made visiting him in hospital fun."

We both nod, hands clasped in front of us, like some sort of mirror—action game.

"Are you seeing anyone?" he asks.

I want to say, *And your grandfather loved how polite you always are asking after people* but instead I lie. "Yes, no, well … you know, sort of, it's … (and here I shrug) … early days."

"Yeah, me too."

I don't really want to hear that so I listen for any other sound floating around the room, which happens to be the horse—woman saying, "I'm only becoming a doctor so it will make me a better mother." Followed by a trilling bray.

Seth says something else to me — something like well, it's great to see you or have a nice life or please sign the guestbook or I hope you're enjoying the singing lessons I gave you as a breaking—up gift (or maybe he says goodbye gift) — and I nod (again) and he walks through the crowd which shows no sign of leaving, to the other side of the room and sidles up beside horse—woman and slips his arm around her waist.

Hmm, so there's a downside to being able to see better.

"If I don't have a baby soon I think my ovaries are going to burst," horse—woman says to a man in a yarmulke.

A dark suit steps into my line of vision so I bend at the waist and through the crowd, watch horse—woman slip her arm around Seth. He nuzzles his chin into her shoulder and I wish I could dislike her but … they look quite good together. He's a little shorter than her and she's older than him — maybe thirty, maybe she was a nurse before she started studying medicine, or a hair / hat model in a previous life, or a jockey before she grew too tall — but physically they look in proportion.

Still, I wonder what Seth sees in her. And even more so, listening to her conversation and watching her cock her head and drape her sleek and lustrous mane, and pose.

And I wonder what he ever saw in me. Just an older woman pity fu –

"How are you, Susan?"

I turn to see Barry, Grigor's brother, just as he takes a blini from a tray offered by a waitress wearing crisp black and a crisper smile.

"Morgana, I mean Morgana," Barry adds, as the waitress disappears with her tray into the crowd.

Barry, whose high cheekbones on a thin face and short dark hair atop deep brown eyes also remind me of Grigor. Grigor before his plastic surgery. Grigor before he had his nose chiselled and his wrinkles blasted away.

Barry, who I worked for a few months back, in the therapy practice he shares with Grigor and who had appointments with Mr Rubinstein almost every day, which is how I came to know Mr Rubinstein in the first place and how I came to be here at Mr Rubinstein's funeral.

"*Susan* is okay," I say. "It's my real name."

Barry – his mouth full of blini (the half uneaten portion he clasps in his fingers as he waves his hand in the air) – looks at me, eyes shining with new interest. And swallows.

"You're just not a Morgana to me, you're always a Susan. I never worked out why you changed it."

Oh, it was another life ago …

"How's Grigor?" I ask. (God, I can't help myself, I don't *care* how Grigor is yet I still do the polite thing and ask about him.)

"Fuck him, fuck whatever his name is even if he is my twin," Barry says. "Fuck him if he's just got out of prison. How are *you*? *Really*, I mean. I want to know: how are you *really*?"

And now the blini and napkin are on the piano beside my empty teacup and he's flinging his hands in the air.

"I mean, I'm a little late for the wedding rehearsal and suddenly I'm not best man any longer and you're not matron of honour and the wedding is off and I'm told you've resigned your admin job at the practice and I have no idea what's happened and I really enjoyed having you in the office ..."

I smile. His intense unblinking gaze might put some people off but I've always liked that about him, even when he was my brother–in–law, even when Grigor was still called Greg. And Barry's enthusiastic hand–waving is infectious, another mirror–game. I'm stirring the air too and I don't know why.

"... and now here you are," he adds, with a sigh and a smile, "ready to tell me."

I don't know what to tell him.

"But it's old news, isn't it?" Barry says. "*Old* news." He picks up what's left of the blini and the napkin from the piano and looks around the room. Perhaps Jewish funerals are popular, because the room is still full, and shows no signs of emptying soon. Even with heartbreak, I think, something can be learned.

"I guess Mr Rubinstein must have been one of your favourite patients," I say.

"Favourite patient?" Barry says. "God no, he was my favourite *bookie*." He laughs, like he's been caught with his hand in the biscuit jar and is trying to charm his way out with disarming honesty. "And not a great bookie either but he was a nice man and nice men his age and with his life experience are few and far between."

I nod. And Barry waves his hands in the air a little more.

"But he was never my patient, he was too switched–on for psychotherapy."

I nod again, just as I see the horse–woman pass behind Barry, swiping the straw hat from her head as she smiles. And there I see it, in broad daylight, or as broad as daylight gets inside well–attended funeral refreshments at a well–appointed funeral home: her very own racing stripe, dark brown regrowth through the blonde mane.

A smile spreads across my face. Somehow that regrowth makes me feel better.

Gabrielle

by Gary Percesepe

Wednesday, 26th November 2014

We cross into New Mexico on US 84. After Durango, Gabrielle talks nonstop. About her ex, who is hooked up in some bad business — some high—wall white—collar Greenwich crime that I can't quite fathom. About her bitch goddess magazine editor with the signature blunt cut. She talks about Andrew, who had rented the Range Rover in Denver and driven the three of them to New Mexico for Anna's Thanksgiving Break from NYU, only to leave them there because of some business deal he had to wrap up in New York. Which is how she and Anna happened to be in Telluride on the night I met Anna at The Last Dollar Saloon, after I had finished my dinner with Henry and Kate. Andrew is being re—evaluated, Gabrielle says. She talks about her job in the city and how she was coming to dread it, and her days as a rocker and her nights out with Deborah Harry and her Blondie mates.

Two things happen as she talks on past 2 am. Three things, if you count me trying to calculate where in the hell we are going. First, I miss Anna. And second, I begin to understand where Anna comes from. Gabrielle is funny, tough, and beautiful. She's whip—smart, cutting, ironic, and very New York. She doesn't ask about Anna, which I appreciate. She does ask about Frankie. For the fourth or fifth time this Thanksgiving week I try to explain, and get exhausted. I throw up my hands. She doesn't interrupt. She gives me that.

She takes her eyes off the road to look at me. Then makes the dual motions for zip the lip.

We drive. I study the pavement. The road looks more and more attractive. I like how it lies there, mile after mile, year after year, how it serves the needs of others without complaint, the traveling citizenry, how it sees everything, but from its limited perspective. It's road. It knows what it is and doesn't try to be anything more than that. It's variable. It sticks to earth, or is suspended above water. It doesn't care about us, but still makes itself available.

At two thirty we enter the mineral springs resort at Ojo Caliente, not far from Taos. Gabrielle reaches into her purse and produces a key to a cliffside suite. "I never checked out," she says. I nod and head for the bathroom, rubbing my eyes.

She raps on the door and hands me a swimsuit. "It's Andrew's. He left in a hurry. You're the same size," she says.

It's a black Speedo and a perfect fit. I find a robe hung on the door and put that on too. She throws me some flip flops.

Gabrielle hooks her arm through mine. We walk outside, into the clear New Mexico night. The door seals shut behind us. Our flip flops slap the pathway. She wears a black bikini under her robe, and carries her purse on her high shoulders.

We enter a large iron pool. There is not a soul in sight. The warm water bubbles up beneath us, rising upward from an underground vault. A massive rock looms over our heads. We shed our robes and dip beneath the steaming surface of the water.

Gabrielle reaches back to dig in her purse. She tells me to open my mouth, and then places what looks like a brown earthen button on my tongue and tells me to swallow. I do.

"What is it?" I ask.

"Peyote." She swallows a button, and fastens her purse.

"Fuck, Gabrielle, what's this shit gonna do?"

"Relax. Slide back into it, Gary. You have to trust me, OK?"

We sit there and soak, studying our skin. She takes one of my hands in hers. We are three handed. Our hands have tiny clear bubbles on them. I look over at her and nod.

"Native American legend tells that the giant rock guards the place where the ancient people of the mesa once received food and water during times of famine. It's said that the iron in this pool prevents fatigue. It's considered beneficial to the blood, and to your immune system."

We lie back, braced against the side of the pool, and look at the stone citadel thrust upward into the starry night. It looks like the Acropolis, a miniature city in stone. We take it in, our necks stretched up like tourists at the twin towers in lower Manhattan. Off in the distance a coyote barks. Our four legs, crooked in the water below, rest on the pebbled floor.

"I could use some immunity," I say.

Gabrielle laughs. "If you're referring to Anna, relax," she says. "I encouraged her."

I raise an eyebrow.

"I trust her judgment."

"You do?" I ponder this.

"Of course, she's my daughter."

"So how'd she do?"

Gabrielle punches my upper arm. "She did fine. She made a good choice. You're harmless, Gary."

"Thanks," I say. "I think?"

"My ex may not see it that way, of course."

We bump hips like salsa dancers under the slippery water, and she smiles. Anna was right, she has cover girl teeth. I like the way the skin of her mouth moves. Her lips part slowly, pulling up her cheekbones slightly.

"In Italy, the age of consent is sixteen," she says.

"Ah, Italia."

"Besides, I was fourteen when I made it the first time," she says.

"Four years younger than me," I say. And seven years older than Anna, I start to say, then check myself, figuring that Gabrielle knows how old her daughter is.

"I was in Italy, actually. In Venice, with a museum guide at the Gallerie dell'Accademia, while my parents were gamboling. His name was Francesco, oddly enough. He took me to a back room where they were restoring a Tintoretto."

"I was in America," I say. "At prom. At a Westchester country club. I came in my cummerbund."

Our laughter echoes off the rock. I feel my heart rate speeding up. The water, or the peyote, is making me perspire. My skin feels slick and metallic. Underwater, Gabrielle places one foot on top of mine. She has long narrow feet, like Anna's, minus the black toenail polish.

"You've got feet like Anna's," I say. I think about that a minute. The peyote is slowing me down. "Oops. That didn't come out right, and is probably inappropriate. Hers are like yours, I mean."

"Yours are hairy," she says.

"I forgot to shave."

"There's only hair on top of your feet, I hope."

"Far as I know." I pull my wrinkled foot up to eye level. It takes some effort. I let it plop back into the water. She reaches over and grabs it, pulls it into her watery lap.

Gabrielle sits up straighter in the pool. She let's go of my hand. She waits until our eyes make full contact.

"Anna likes you, Gary. You do understand that, right?"

"I do," I say.

"And you like her too," she asks.

"Very much," I say.

Gabrielle twirls her hair a second. Then she stands to her feet, and pulls me up with her.

"See," she says. "That's what we've got to work on."

Gabrielle steers me over to an old pump. She places a hand at the back of my neck, pushing my head down, and then pulls the pump handle. Water pools at my feet. She guides my head under the flowing water. I drink deeply.

"This is the Lithia spring," she says.

When I've had enough she takes a long drink herself. We look back at the lighted pools, shimmering. Everything is lovely in the pale light of stars and moon.

Gabrielle steers me back to the room. We walk carefully. "The lithium," she says, "relieves depression and aids digestion."

We reach the room. I collapse on the bed. I see Gabrielle pour herself a pretty drink in a heavy glass. She opens wide the windows. A light breeze blows cool against my fevered skin. The breeze blows the curtains. I close my eyes and see sunken tubs with copper fixtures, linen rugs from Arabia, the red mountains of Sangre de Christo, the lemon trees of Capri waving against the azure sky.

I wake at first light. Sitting next to me in the ruined bed is Gabrielle. She sits with her back against the wrought iron headboard in a black lace bra and unzipped jeans, smoking. She stares into the middle distance and listens, I am guessing, to the gentle beating of a drum, coming from somewhere outside.

This may be a dream. Or not an actual dream, but surely something with dreamlike features? A small bird flits in and out of the open window. At the base of the window lies a suitcase of snow. A twisted strip of bed sheet is knotted around my ankle. Gabrielle sits smoking more peyote. I hear her lungs work. It is snowing outside, and then it isn't.

Samford Tries to Die
by Nathaniel Tower

Thursday, 27th November 2014

On a Thursday in November, Samford ingests what might be a lethal dose of Drain–O.

He downs half the bottle, which, if the bottle is any indicator, is way more than enough to kill him.

He does not call the emergency number for immediate attention.

Samford's consumption of the thick drain declogger is not performed by accident. Nor is it an act of homicide. It isn't necessarily an act of suicide either. It's more of a "let's see what happens" sort of thing.

Based on all the crazy shit he's experienced in the past ten months, he expects anything could happen.

Not that he necessarily *wants* to be saved. Dying wouldn't be the worst thing that could happen to him. After all, it would put an end to the rapidly exploding population of Samford clones. Samford just can't keep his dick in his pants. It's almost as if every woman on Earth is trained to fuck Samford as soon as his genitals have reloaded enough sperm to impregnate them. Samford recalls a biology teacher in high school informing the class it only takes one sperm for this miracle to occur. Samford sees nothing miraculous about it.

Within five minutes of swallowing the last gulp of Drain—O, there is a knock on Samford's door. He expects the clone police, or some crazy ass clone doctor, or maybe something incredibly odd, not that anything would be odd to him anymore.

But instead of seeing something batshit nuts, he sees Sarah — or at least *a* Sarah — standing in the doorway of the fly—by—night hotel room.

"I finally found you," she says. Samford instantly knows it is her, the real Sarah, which must mean it isn't the real Sarah, especially since *his* real Sarah is a clone, or at least claims to be one — and since he could never find a serial number in all his hours spelunking in her asshole, she must be a clone. It's too confusing for him to even think about, especially with the Drain—O starting to rip away his insides. It doesn't really matter though. He knows he will fuck this woman until another Samford bursts forth from her vagina. Maybe it will be a mutant Samford.

"You aren't the right Sarah," Samford spits through the gargling slobber that is forming in his mouth.

"Of course I am," she says as she takes his convulsing hand. "I can prove it to you."

"How?" Pain radiates in his stomach and he wonders if this pain is what the women feel before they give birth to the full—grown Samfords.

She puts her finger on his lips, sealing off the bubbles of foam. "Just be quiet and let me show you."

Samford stands still and doesn't say a word while the Sarah slowly kneels to the floor and slides down his pants. Even in a dying state, he knows that sex will overcome the seething anger and disgust he holds at the sight of this imposter Sarah. For a brief second, he also hopes it will feel the pain.

The Sarah blows on his penis, then bites at the air. Samford thinks this is something from a really shitty porno movie, something called *Clone Fucking* or *Clones Giving Blow Jobs*. The type of porno movie that doesn't even use a clever title. If

Samford is going to die while getting head, he wants it to be something from an A—list porn movie.

But the Sarah is not interested in sucking his dick. After two more puffs of air — which have elicited a raging hard—on — she says, "Now bend over and let me show you I'm the real Sarah."

What happens next is something Samford would rather not anyone ever know. He bends over, prepared to accept his fate. What the Sarah does is magical, but before Samford can fully enjoy it, he drops to the floor, thick green bubbles bursting from his wide—open mouth and onto the filthy hotel carpet.

Welcome Home, Jacaranda
by Kimberlee Smith

Friday, 28th November 2014

I'm naming my half–sister Jacaranda, after my favorite flowering tree. Jacaranda has been with me for a month to the day and, like me and my daughter Etheline, she didn't have a chance to meet her mum nor for her mum to meet her. She was stillborn and her mum, who was close to death herself whilst giving birth to Jackie's brother — they were twins but only the boy was born alive — didn't have a moment to even see Jackie before my dad, Brother Tom Bend, hoisted her lifeless body into the air, praising God for delivering to them an angel. Brother Tom stepped right into his evangelical mode of preaching to deflect what was really going on, right there, right then.

Jacaranda came to me; not as a gift from Heaven, but as a gift from Earth. My husband Dean is sulky about the new addition to our family. Ever since his buddies, those German Tourists, left — to spiritual levels unknown — his energy is stormy and unpredictable. Today he's distracting me from the wee one by whinging how lovely it would be if we could just zip up to Heaven together. We two, not with Jacaranda.

"For Christ's sake, Melodie," he pleads, "we've been hanging around here in limbo long enough. There's got to be something more than this … remember what Doreen said when she passed through?"

"Doreen was a horrid spirit. I got a very bad feeling from her," I counter. "Why are you so desperate to leave? I feel more fulfilled than I have since we died. We can look over our flesh—and—bone bub and also have Jacaranda here with us." I feel Jacaranda lean into me, warm me, soothe me. The storm that usually builds up when I lose my temper is a steady breeze with mist … no thunder, no downpour, no blizzard, no tornado. Jacaranda steadies me. But Jacaranda will never know what it is to be a baby. All she knows is the womb. Having been pregnant with Etheline, Jacaranda and I have a symbiotic relationship.

I think that perhaps if I were to agree to travel to Heaven or somewhere like it — maybe our marriage will be perfect, our problems will disappear, our worries and miscommunications will turn into a blissful, harmonious fusion of love. Like how life was during our first years together. But I feel such a strong pull to Etheline in the living world and to Jacaranda in this afterworld that I cannot risk losing that for a chance of improving my marriage: I am dead. My husband is dead. And finally our marriage is dead. When all you have is a spiritual connection to someone and that perishes, there is nothing left.

"Come on, baby, let's go. This here bub isn't ours. She isn't even a real baby, for fuck's sake! She don't need to be changed or fed or nothing. She's dead. Don't you get it?"

As Dean does when he gets in a snit, his aura is changing from a dull stone color, which is mainly what it is these days, to a flickering like a telly with bad reception. Before the flickering felt like static with intermittent drum beats to me; his unnerved spirit was usually sharp and simple. Today it has weakened to a sluggish flicker, like energy draining from a corroded battery, and the drum beats are more like faraway echoes, traveling across mountain ranges through soupy fog. Dean's not going to give in.

"I don't mean to be harsh, but you never took care of a *live* infant. I was the one who did. Your mum, she spent a fair amount of time helping out, but I was the parent. Not you. You never even met her. You don't even know her. You're creating a situation in your emotional mind that just can't exist. You never met her, which, I am sorry to have to tell you, is proof positive you can't possibly love her. It's a fantasy, babe. For the sake of you and me, give it up."

"My *emotional* mind? As opposed to the mind that was housed in a bone cage, in a swirl of gray matter, before your snake bit me? Chewed on me until it killed me? You're the one who's lost his mind."

He ignores me by shutting down the thoughts I've put out there for him to absorb. He's in deep denial. We never had these complicated issues when we were alive. Or maybe we did but I was the one ignoring the warning signs. Sex made up for all the shortcomings in our relationship. Regardless, I'm not leaving either of my bubs.

I know when you die, time stops. I know Jacaranda will never grow up. I know she's not a real baby, but she's all I've got. She will never play peek–a–boo with me, like Etheline does with Mum. She won't smile when she sees me. She will never open her eyes. She knew nothing of the world, and as I feel her with me, the difference is so clear between life and death. The only one here who got a taste of what it's like to love and be loved on earth, to be held and to hold, is Dean. This is as close as Jacaranda and I are going to get to that.

Having Jacaranda with me is like being pregnant again. I'll never know what it's like to raise a child, but one thing I do know about Jacaranda being here is that she can feel the only world she ever knew, and I can remain in this glorious state of what it feels like to have a baby inside me, forgetting where I am now and feeling the anticipation of being a mum. Dean is not taking this away from me. Not again.

"I got you loud and clear. You're thinking it was all my fault. I kept those snakes as securely and responsibly as I possibly could have." He moans and turns blackly iridescent, like when oil and rainwater mix.

"Damn straight. It was your carelessness keeping them in the house when I was fully pregnant in the first place."

Jacaranda is hiding in me now; her spirit is burrowing like she's afraid. I let her in. It's like I'm full of life again, but that's only because it's what I wish. Two spirits together are strong. Sacred. Dean and I never felt this close, in life or in death.

"You sure didn't complain about moving out of your mum's old caravan and into a home of our own, with air conditioning and waterbeds and everything. You know I worked my ass off to provide those things for you *and* your mum."

Jacaranda shudders, just like the trees do when a wild wind kicks up.

"She ain't my baby. She ain't your baby. All we three got in common is we're dead," Dean says.

I've heard enough. He's free to go. I don't think there's anything, or anywhere, better than this place for a spirit turned bad like Dean's. Difference between the two of us is that he wants to know what else is out there, but I'm afraid to know. Jacaranda is right here with me. While I'm thinking hard about us, and our situation, I stop to realize that Dean has gone.

Nobody, Somebody
by Vanessa Weibler Paris

Saturday, 29th November 2014

"You're nobody 'til somebody loves you," I hum quietly as I pull open the refrigerator door.

The air inside the refrigerator buzzes, *hmmmm–hmmmm–click–click* on repeat. Its bright white sides are studded with drops of condensation, concave holes, perfect little mounds like candy buttons on paper tape. I trace them with the darts of my eyes, drawing zigzags and diamonds and finally a star.

The shelves are filled with nothing but bottles of water.

"Close it," says Iris. "Close it. Close it!" It becomes a single word.

I am Iris's muse. Her love. Her art. Her exhibit.

There's no more food for me now, just water. I must become thinner: Iris' art has *clean lines*. But I keep forgetting, keep going back for the food.

"Close it!" she repeats.

The condensation drops are warming now, stretching and tearing. Some start to roll down the sides, snail–trailing into neat vertical stripes like overlapping prison bars. A bulb flickers in the back.

A housefly coasts in smoothly, landing on a white bottlecap, expiration–dated far beyond my own. Its eyes shimmer red. The fly buzzes in competition with the cooling system, trying to win a battle the fridge isn't even fighting.

My leg is bleeding again. The bandage Rorschachs in slowly seeping shapes. I stare at a big blot of red: is it a head of lettuce? a lotus pod?

"I just need to know how deep it is," Iris had said last night, razor blade in her fist. "Until I hit bone."

"The exhibit?" I asked.

"The exhibit," she said.

I take out a bottle, try to open it. Iris grabs it from me, cracks it with a quick twist. I lift the bottle, gratefully, and sip. She slams the fridge shut.

"I'm going out for a bit," Iris calls over her shoulder, heading for the door, and then she's gone. She's gone a lot lately. It seems. Or maybe it's just that I'm sleeping more.

When I was in school, they used to say that everyone should drink eight glasses of water per day. I'm not sure that's true any longer. It's like the Four Basic Food Groups or catching a cold from being damp and chilled, the science that was shoved down our throats and then later quietly discarded.

I finish my water, open another, and gulp. I'm feeling stronger now. Fuller. If I grow, though, Iris will leave me, and I'll be alone again. I'll be Slim Jim again, poor pitied Slim Jim, who has family and friends and co-workers who love him but nothing more.

I throw my empty to the floor, where Iris won't like it. Open another.

I once read an article on what it's like to drown. At first you panic, try to hold your breath. That goes on for a while. When you can't hold out any longer, water gushes in. Your lungs feel like they're tearing and burning, but that doesn't last long. Finally, you feel calm and tranquil, then go slowly unconscious. Your heart stops, and finally, your brain dies.

What time is it? The wall clock is gone.

I can feel myself gaining weight as I continue to drink. It hurts to swallow, and makes a hard noise in my throat, *nnunnk nnunnk nnunnk*. I pick up the phone and dial.

"I'd like to request a song," I tell the woman who answers the phone at the radio station. "It's by Dean Martin." I open a bottle of water, leaving the refrigerator door ajar. But they don't accept requests now, haven't for years.

I feel like vomiting, but I breathe and I breathe and it passes.

I take another, open it with shaking hands.

The red-eyed fly buzzes in tune with the song in my mind. "*You're nobody 'til somebody looooooooves youuuuuuuuuu.*"

Close it, I can hear Iris saying, and so I do. Maybe I'll let the fly out in a bit, see if it can come back to life. Or maybe I'll leave it there, dying slowly, without even realizing.

Sunday Brunch

by Joanne Jagoda

Sunday, 30th November 2014

"Mom, what time are they coming?"

"They'll be here around eleven. I need you to pick up some eggs. I thought I had more, but I only have a half dozen. I hope the guys will like mushroom omelets."

"They will Mom, and no one can resist your home—style potatoes. The onions browning in the butter smell so good. "

"Oh, Cass … forgot to tell you and Rob. After brunch, we're going to the De Young Museum. I got us tickets for the Impressionist exhibit. It's supposed to be fabulous."

"Count Rob and me out."

"We'll talk about that later. Get going. I need those eggs."

"I'll get her lazy butt up."

I want to pinch myself. I've been on a roller coaster since January. Just like Eli said, Sandy called me on Halloween. Who would ever believe that a Mossad agent could be a matchmaker. He had a feeling we would be right for each other. I know he felt badly about how I was used by Damon Southeby, because he saw it all happening but couldn't do anything about it.

125

When Sandy came to the door he had a cute smile that crinkled his eyes. He wasn't drop–dead gorgeous but nice looking, built solid and taller than me. He was checking me out and I was glad I got my hair cut and looked good in my new burgundy sweater.

We went to my favorite pizza place, Tomaso's in North Beach. We talked so much over our pizza and bottle of Chianti that the waiters were piling the chairs on tops of the tables until we got the hint. Then we picked up ice cream and ate it in the kitchen standing up at the counter. We felt comfortable like we've known each other forever and laughed until two in the morning. I insisted he not drive home, and he slept in the guest room. The next morning he left quietly. Breakfast would have been too much too soon. He got that.

We've been seeing each other often. Bike riding, movies; I cook dinner or we take long walks. And we've spent one yummy weekend at a quaint Bed and Breakfast in Half Moon Bay. He's a sweet lover. It's only been one month, but it feels like a lifetime with him.

I was tickled when Sandy said he wanted to be with us for Thanksgiving. He came over early on Thursday and helped with chopping. He carved the turkey too. His son was with his wife's parents, which was fine. The girls had just come home from school. At first it was strained. They were civil but quiet and not themselves. I know they don't want me to get hurt again. I'm touched by that. After my horrible experience with that liar, Damon, they are acting like guard dogs.

"Why are you sitting on me, Cass? Leave me alone."

"Rob, get your butt out of bed and come with me to Safeway. Mom needs eggs."

"Oooohh … I had way too much to drink last night. My head is pounding."

"No one told you to down three margaritas. You over–did it, Rob."

"I can figure that out for myself, Cass. I'm the one feeling like shit."

"Sandy and his son are coming for brunch."

"I don't want to make small talk. I feel like crap."

"Rob, I'll get you some Peet's Columbian, the best hangover cure. I'm excited for Mom. Sandy seems real. He's going bald; his pants were falling the other night. In some ways he reminds me of Dad. When he was carving the turkey for Thanksgiving I had a flash of how Dad used to do it."

"I know what you mean, Cass. He feels comfortable and he's funny. I loved when he was telling stories about some of the weird women he's met through online dating."

"Rob, do you think he and Mom have a future?"

"I don't know, but I feel better about him compared to that other jerk–off. He was too smooth, too good–looking, I didn't trust him from the start."

"Yeah, well you were right. Come on, get dressed and let's go."

"All right all right."

"*Cass and Rob, I need those eggs.*"

"*YEAH MOM, we'll be right down.*"

"Smells *delish*, Mom." Cass grabs a chunk of pineapple from the bowl.

"Kids, pick me up a sour cream and make it two dozen eggs. Robin, sunglasses in the house?"

"It's bright in here. Mom, anything else? Tell us now …"

"No, that's it."

§

I wonder where the girls are with the eggs. I bet they stopped for coffee. Rob must have another hangover. I want to go away again with Sandy. Our weekend at the B&B was perfect. It all just feels right with him. I hope the girls will like Josh. I better finish setting the table. Where are my blue placemats? Oh, here's my favorite picture of the four of us in Maui on the beach.

Paul, I've met a good man. He's a lot like you. Give me your blessing.

Finally they're back. "Thanks kids. Leave the eggs on the counter."

"Mom, we were talking. Do you like Sandy? I mean really like him?"

I was afraid they might ask me. I need to crack these eggs in the bowl. Where's the salt and pepper? They come out better when I use a whisk. Got to grate the cheddar. Mushrooms are cleaned and washed. I'll assemble everything for the omelets.

Cassie watches me whisk the eggs. "Mom, you didn't answer. We want to know."

"Well, if you must know, it hasn't been very long, but I do like him … a lot. I think it's even more than that. I feel like it is the beginning of something good we can grow in to."

The girls come over to me and we hug and hold on to each other. We've been through an ordeal that is all too fresh. "No sweats guys, puh—lease???"

"Yeah, yeah."

Robin can be such a brat. I'm going to finish the potatoes. It's ten minutes to eleven. They'll be here soon.

§

"You guys look nice and jeans are way better than sweats. There's the bell. Rob, get the door."

"I see Josh through the window. He's cute. Looks like Sandy but taller."

"Hi Sandy. Mom, Cass, Sandy and Josh ARE HEE … RE!"

"Hey, Anne." He gives me a hug and peck on the cheek. The three kids are embarrassed. Then he bows at the waist like a gallant knight, and they laugh.

"Donaldson Ladies, meet my son, Josh. Josh, meet the Donaldson Ladies."

I'm relieved Sandy broke the ice. "Come on everyone. Let's hit the table. Just tell me what you want in your made–to–order omelets. Cassie, serve the home fries. Robin, bring the fruit salad to the table."

We eat and laugh and I quietly observe the three kids talking about school, football and music. Sandy grabs my hand under the table and squeezes.

"More home fries, Josh?" He hands me his plate.

"They definitely don't serve these on campus." He continues the heated football discussion he was having with Robin. "You know that the 49'ers are going to make it to the playoffs and the Super Bowl."

Robin shakes her head, "No way, Josh. The Seahawks are going all the way and would you like to make a little bet?"

Sandy pipes in, "Don't do it, Josh. She knows what she's talking about."

§

After brunch everyone helps clear the table, then the twins and Josh head upstairs. I hear noise and arguing but it sounds like they are having fun. I let my breath out. "I think they are getting along well, Sandy."

"I knew they would." He puts his arms around me at the sink. I turn and kiss him full on the lips, dripping soap bubbles on his sweater. We don't hear them walk into the kitchen.

Josh clears his throat. We break apart, and Sandy whistles like we've been caught making out by our parents.

Robin takes the car keys from the counter. "Mom, we don't want to go to the de Young. Got other plans. Hope you won't mind. Now, you two behave ..."

We smile and Sandy answers before I can, reading my mind. "That's fine. See you later." The door slams.

It feels like a cyclone left the house with a whoosh. Sandy helps me dry the rest of the dishes. It's a rare quiet moment, and though we don't speak, we recognize something special is taking place between us. I feel a rare contentment that I haven't experienced in a long time.

I dry my hands on a kitchen towel and Sandy leads me to the sofa. He massages my feet in my socks. I don't need to ask if he wants to stay and hang out at home. We curl up on the sofa with the Sunday paper. The Impressionists can wait for another day.

Authors

Rachel Ambrose

is a twenty—something fiction writer from Connecticut. Her favorite season is winter, she enjoys well—made Manhattans, and she loves Southern fiction. Her work has appeared in *Crack the Spine*, *Exiles Literary Magazine*, and *The Colton Review*. She is currently at work on her second novel and she blogs at http://victorywhiskeyjuliet.tumblr.com.

Lynn Beighley

is a fiction writer stuck in a technical book writer's body. Her stories often involve deeply flawed characters and the unsatisfying meshing of the virtual and actual world. She has an MFA in Creative Writing and currently has 16 books published.

Margaret Bingel

is just a writer, living in Manchester, New Hampshire. She spends her time working at her father's beer store, art modeling, and writing (when she can). She doesn't have a website or a blog yet, but who knows, maybe she'll have one in the future.

Guilie Castillo–Oriard

is a Mexican writer currently exiled in the island of Curaçao. She misses Mexican food and Mexican *amabilidad*, but the laissez–faire attitude and the beaches of the Caribbean are fair exchange. Plus, the bounty of cultural diversity inspires great culture–clash fiction. Guilie is currently revising and editing her first novel. Her short stories have appeared in *Fiction 365*, *Lady Ink Magazine* and *Pure Slush*. She blogs at http://guilie–castillo–oriard.blogspot.com.

John Wentworth Chapin

lives and writes in Baltimore, where he is too frequently starting Project B before finishing Project A. John writes non–fiction as well as fiction. Find him at http://johnwentworthchapin.com.

James Claffey

hails from County Westmeath, Ireland, and lives on an avocado ranch in Carpinteria, CA with his family. He is the author of a collection of short fiction, *Blood a Cold Blue*. His website can be found at http://jamesclaffey.com.

Gay Degani

has published online and in print including *The Best of Every Day Fiction* editions and her own collection, *Pomegranate Stories*. She is the founder–editor emeritus of EDF's *Flash Fiction Chronicles*, a staff editor at *Smokelong Quarterly*, and blogs at http://wordsinplace.blogspot.com where a list of her work can be found. She's had two stories nominated for Pushcart consideration and won the eleventh Annual Glass Woman Prize for her flash piece, *Something about L.A.*

Michelle Elvy

is an editor and writer who has meandered from the shores of the Chesapeake to New Zealand's Bay of Islands. Michelle has published poetry, short stories and non−fiction about travel, faraway places, food, motorcycling, slow travel, the kindness of strangers and raising children in unusual places for numerous literary journals and magazines in the US, Canada, Australasia, the UK and Europe. She edits at *Flash Frontier: An Adventure in Short Fiction* and *Blue Five Notebook*. She can also be found regularly at *Awkword Paper Cut*. More about manuscript assessment and Michelle's take on editing and writing can be found at http://michelleelvy.com.

Gloria Garfunkel

is a psychologist and writer with a Ph.D. from Harvard University in Psychology and Social Relations. A former psychotherapist, she has published many stories in literary journals and anthologies.

Teresa Burns Gunther

has had fiction and non−fiction appear in numerous literary journals and most recently in *Northwind Magazine*, *Bookslut* and *Best New Writing 2012*. Teresa is the Editor of *The Lakeside*, an online literary magazine, and she founded Lakeshore Writers Workshop in Oakland, California where she leads creative writing workshops and classes and works one−on−one with writers. You can find more information and links to her work at http://www.teresaburnsgunther.com/.

Gill Hoffs

lives with her family and an ever−dwindling supply of Nutella in the North of England. Find Gill on Facebook or as @gillhoffs on twitter, email her a dirty joke at gillhoffs@hotmail.co.uk, or leave a clean comment at http://gillhoffs.wordpress.com/. *Wild: a collection* was published by *Pure Slush Books* in 2012. Her non–fiction book *The Sinking of RMS Tayleur: the Lost Story of the Victorian Titanic* is out now from *Pen & Sword*. Feel free to send her chocolate.

Joanne Jagoda

of Oakland, California, took an inspiring writing workshop after retiring in 2009, and launched on a long–postponed creative writing journey. Since discovering her passion for writing, she has worked non–stop on short stories, poetry and non–fiction. Her work has appeared in a number of e–zines and print anthologies, including *Pure Slush* and *Idea Gems Magazine*, and she was a poet of the month for a Jewish news weekly in Northern California. When not taking writing and poetry classes, Joanne enjoys being a writer–coach for ninth graders, Zumba, and visiting her three grandchildren in Jerusalem.

Len Kuntz

is a writer from Washington State and an editor at the (currently on hiatus) online literary magazine *Metazen*. His work appears widely in print and online, and you can find more of his work at http://lenkuntz.blogspot.com.

Sally–Anne Macomber

was born and raised in Toronto, Canada, and studied journalism at Concordia University in Montreal. Her work on high fashion and the demise of haute couture has appeared in various online and print publications in both Europe and North America. She turned to writing flash fiction in 2010, and hasn't looked back.

Jessica McHugh

is an author of speculative fiction that spans the genre from horror and alternate history to epic fantasy. A member of the Horror Writers Association and a 2013 Pulp Ark nominee, she has devoted herself to novels, short stories, poetry, and playwriting. Jessica has had thirteen books published in five years, including the bestselling *Rabbits in the Garden, The Sky: The World* and the gritty coming–of–age thriller, *PINS*. More info on her speculations and publications can be found at http://www.jessicamchughbooks.com.

Gwendolyn Joyce Mintz

is a fiction writer and aspiring photographer. Her work has appeared in various online and print publications. In other incarnations, Mintz is a writing instructor, a teddy bear maker and somebody's grandmother.

Mandy Nicol

grew up in Melbourne, Australia and made a tree change to country Victoria in the mid–nineties – the decade, not her age. She has various animals including a flockette of pet sheep that are thankful for her vegaquarian habits. She writes short stories and loves flash fiction. *Pure Slush* is the first venue to publish her work.

Derek Osborne

lives in eastern Pennsylvania. His work has appeared in *Boston Literary Magazine, Bartleby Snopes, Literary Orphans, The Linnet's Wings, Pure Slush* and many others. To read more visit http://gertrudesflat.blogspot.com, or you can email him at derekosborne1@gmail.com.

Vanessa Weibler Paris

lives in Erie, Pa., with a guy, a girl, a boy, a bunny rabbit and a dog. She writes things both real (for work) and pretend (for fun). Her favorite things include hot peppers, bad puns, small—world stories, and tales with a twist at the end.

Gary Percesepe

is Associate Editor at *New World Writing* (formerly *Mississippi Review*) and a Contributor at *The Nervous Breakdown*. Author of four books in philosophy, Percesepe's poetry, fiction, essays, and interviews have appeared in *Story Quarterly, N + 1, Salon, Mississippi Review, The Millions, Brevity, PANK, Metazen, The Brooklyner,* and other places. His collection of short stories, *Why I Did the Grocery Girl,* is forthcoming from Aqueous Books. His poetry collection *falling* and his flash fiction collection *itch* were published by *Pure Slush Books* in late 2013. He has taught at Saint Louis University, Wittenberg University, and University of Dayton. He lives in Buffalo, New York.

Matt Potter

is an Australian—born writer who keeps a part of his psyche in Berlin. Matt has been published in various places online, and he is, rather amazingly, also the founding editor of *Pure Slush*. You can find more of his work at http://mattcpotter.webs.com/.

Darryl Price

was born in Kentucky and educated at Thomas More College. A founding member of L. Jack Roth's Yellow Pages Poets, he has published dozens of chapbooks, and his poems have appeared in many journals. He currently edits *Olentangy Review* with his wife Melissa.

Stephen V. Ramey

is an American author from New Castle, Pennsylvania. His work has appeared in many places, including *The Doctor TJ Eckleburg Review*, *The Journal of Compressed Creative Arts*, and *A Capella Zoo*. *Glass Animals*, his first collection of (very) short fiction is available from *Pure Slush Books*. Find him and more of his work at his website: http://www.stephenvramey.com.

Shane Simmons

is a self—confessed coffee shop writer who believes that regardless of quality, each paragraph penned should be rewarded with sweet treats (cake, muffins, Belgian waffles, etc). London—born, he ran away to Glasgow ten years ago. Since then he has expanded his waistline, and you can read his blog at http://scribblingsimmons.wordpress.com/.

Kimberlee Smith

is a writer whose poetry, essays, fiction, and creative non—fiction have been published in numerous literary journals and anthologies. She was awarded a residency to the Jentel Arts Program in 2013. She received her MA in English from the University of Sydney, a certificate in the Creative Writing Program through UCLA, and her BA in Journalism from the University of Southern California. She can do a headstand on a trampoline, kill a chook, and make hard cider from the apples in her orchard.

Andrew Stancek

was born in Bratislava and saw Russian tanks occupying his homeland. His dreams of circuses and ice cream, flying and lion—taming, miracle and romance have appeared in print in *LA Review*, *Windsor Review* and *New Sun Rising: Stories for Japan*. Among the many online publications featuring his work are *Every Day Fiction, Gemini Magazine* (Flash Fiction Contest Grand Prize Winner), *fwriction, r.kv.r.y. quarterly literary journal, Tin House, Flash Fiction Chronicles, The Linnet's Wings, Connotation Press, THIS Literary Magazine, LA Review, Windsor Review, Thrice Fiction Magazine, New Sun Rising,* and *Pure Slush.*

S usan T epper

is the author of four published books of fiction and a chapbook of poetry. Her most recent title *The Merrill Diaries* (*Pure Slush Books,* July 2013) is a Novel in Stories that follow a young woman's adventures in love and lust on two continents, spanning a decade. Tepper has received nine Pushcart nominations, and one for the Pulitzer Prize in fiction. You can visit her website here: http://www.susantepper.com.

N athaniel T ower

lives in the Twin Cities with his wife and daughter. After teaching high school English for nine years, he decided to pursue a career in writing / publishing / editing. His fiction has appeared in over two hundred online and print journals. His first collection of fiction, *Nagging Wives, Foolish Husbands*, was released in 2014 through *Martian Lit*. Nathaniel is the founding and managing editor of *Bartleby Snopes Literary Magazine and Press*. You can find out more about Nathaniel at http://nathanieltower.wordpress.com.

T ownsend W alker

lives in San Francisco. His stories have been published in over fifty literary journals and included in seven anthologies. One story won the SLO NightWriters story contest. Two were nominated for the PEN / O. Henry Award. Four were performed at the New Short Fiction Series in Hollywood. He is associate editor at *Grey Sparrow Journal*. During a career in finance he published three books, on foreign exchange, derivatives and portfolio management. Educated at Georgetown, NYU and Stanford, you can find his website at http://www.townsendwalker.com.

Michael Webb

is continually surprised anyone is interested in what he has to say. He blogs at http://innocentsaccidentshints.blogspot.com.

Other volumes in the *2014* series from Pure Slush

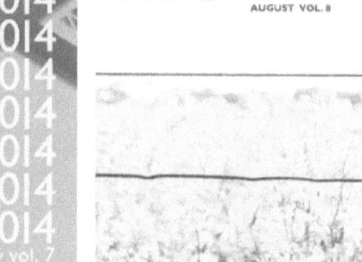

June 2014 Vol. 6
ISBN: 978−1−925101−49−2

July 2014 Vol. 7
ISBN: 978−1−925101−37−9

August 2014 Vol. 8
ISBN: 978−1−925101−40−9

September 2014 Vol. 9
ISBN: 978−1−925101−43−0

October 2014 Vol. 10
ISBN: 978−1−925101−50−8

Dec'ber 2014 Vol. 12
ISBN: 978−1−925101−56−0